THE

MISCHIEVOUS

WIDOW

ZENTS K. SOWUNMI

For additional copies of this or other Zents Sowunmi titles write:

Korloki Publishers Inc.

P.O. Box 316 Shirley NY 11967   Please allow 4 to 6 weeks for delivery.

For bulk orders contact us via email

Korlokipublishers@gmail.com

Don't miss these exciting books from bestselling.

Author

ZENTS KUNLE SOWUNMI

❖ **The Vultures and Vulnerable**

❖ **President Obama: Hero or villain of Capitalism?**

❖ **Unequally Yoking**

❖ **The Secrets of Gabriel**

❖ **Ogun State Policy of Manipulation.**

❖ **Before the Journey Became Home**

❖ **100 ways to Laugh.**

❖ **Cien Maneras de Reir**

❖ **What happened to Our Democracy?**

❖ **Not a stranger Anymore**

Coming soon!!!

❖ **The Loopholes**

❖ **The Covenant Breakers**

❖ **The Return of the Oracle**

❖ **You have my memories.**

Order copies of this author's books directly from www.kpcbooks.com

ZENTS SOWUNMI

THE MISCHIEVOUS WIDOW

KORLOKI

Cover design by:	Korloki Publishers Inc.
Interior design:	Korloki Publishers Inc.
Photographs:	Zents K Sowunmi
Summary:	Thriller and suspense life story
ISBN:	9781936739332
ISBN:	1936739-33-X

PRINTED IN USA

AUTHOR OF THE SECRETS OF GABRIL

ZENTS SOWUNMI

A

NOVEL

The

MISCHIEVUOS WIDOW

The Clash of the gods

KORLOKI: An imprint of Korloki Publishers Inc.,

P. O. Box 316 Shirley NY 11967 USA

PRINTED IN USA

Dedication

To my love

PRAISE FOR the Oracle

Zents Sowunmi *and his books*

Impossible to put down

Library Journal

A Super story   teller of our time

Brooklyn Journals

Oracle Zents is quite a spot to read.

Dada Shokeye

Bronx NY

Smart   and intricate,   with   almost authentic

Characters

The Reporters

Oraclezents writes creatively, depicted through his books.

Chinyere Helyn Njoku

The
MISCHIEVUOS WIDOW

A
NOVEL

Korloki Paperbacks

Special attention

The Stories on history and religions on Africa of this novel were taken from various sources including journals

"There is just one thing you ought to know and abide

with when you meet with the Oracle"

"What is it?"

"Don't tell lies."

"I won't"

"Then I wish you Good luck"

...................Professor Kwame Prapong

PART ONE

Dallas, Texas

1997

Chapter

1

'Ω'Ω'Ω'Ω

"How can I handle life without John?" Marie asked the Oracle.

She was almost in tears in Oracle's Shrine in the State of Texas, her husband, John a professor of international relations from a local University had died inside the swimming Pool while his friend Professor Bimbo, who became deaf and dump when they both tried to save a drowning kid?

Marie Solomon Atilogun began the narration of her pathetic life back in the day in Africa, to the man in his sixties, who the society called "the Oracle" noted for his spiritual powers and traditional wisdom, who just listened with an encouraging look and attention which made it possible for her to pour out her mind effortlessly.

Marie was barely 33 years old when she relocated to the United States of America with her husband, Professor John Solomon Atilogun partially of the Zulu tribe from South Africa, who had secured a teaching appointment in one of the Universities in Canada before he finally relocated to the United States of America.

It was like a bundle of joy for the new couple, the marriage was less than a year, when they were blessed with a son, Mavuso, who arrived three months earlier than usual, they looked forward to a beautiful life of opportunities they would be able to provide for their son in a free society, at least, that was what they were told about the land Columbus and which his children had grabbed from the Red Indians several decades ago, to them, back home in the motherland, it was not a fair deal.

The Republic of Namibia was not as promising as they hoped after independence war led by President Sam Njoma and they hoped the United States of America would give them what would fulfill the dreams of all the years of academic exercises in Africa, and it was never going to be a wasted adventure for them, which was what they hoped for.

The couple's little boy, Mavuso was nice looking with lots of energies, he had too much of his mother in him, with two noticeable dimples on the sides of his cheeks, just like his mother, when he smiled, and it was very infectious, and it captured the attention of everyone around his vicinity.

What a good kid! Everyone was happy with his presence; yes, everyone including the whites in their neighborhood who would not?

The flight to the United States of America in 1997 from Hosea Kutako International Airport, about 45 minutes' drive, East of Windhoek the hub of the National Carrier of the People's Republic of Namibia was not without events.

The Airport was decorated with the photographs of the President Sam Njoma, tucks of Elephant, the flight and all the accolades of it, and somehow, it reminded the couple about the funny side of the movie by Eddie Murphy "Coming to America."

Namibia had gone through a struggle for independence, and it was formerly called Southwest Africa, a country in southern Africa with western border to the Atlantic Ocean.

It also shares land borders with Zambia and Angola to the north, Botswana to the east and South Africa to the south and East.

Although, it does not border Zimbabwe, however less than 200 meters of the Zambezi River, most of the territory became a German Imperial protectorate in 1884 and it remained a German colony until the end of World War I in 1918

When asked why the Germans were interested in the sparsely populated nation of Southwest Africa in the 18th Century, it was revealed, it was as a result of tobacco plantation during the era of slave trade. It has a better taste than any of the products from Cuba

In 1920, the League of Nations mandated the country to South Africa, which imposed its laws and, from 1948, including its apartheid policy which had kept the blacks in the South Africa as hostage to their inheritance.

The port of Walvis Bay and the offshore Penguin Islands had been annexed by the Cape Colony under the British crown by 1878 and had become an integral part of the new Union of South Africa at its creation in 1910.

Uprisings and demands by African leaders led the UN to assume direct responsibility over the territory several decades later. It recognized the Southwest Africa People's Organization (SWAPO) as the official representative of the Namibian people in 1973. Namibia, however, remained under South African administration during that time as South-West Africa.

Following internal violence, South Africa installed an interim administration in Namibia in 1985. Namibia obtained full independence from South Africa in 1990, with the exception of Walvis Bay and the Penguin Islands, which remained under South African control until 1994.

The policy of South Africa then was one of the reasons most people particularly, the academics left the country, and it was the same reason Marie and John her husband with their middle-class education, felt the United States of America would be a fine place for them and their little son Mavuso.

Within ten years, in the State of Texas, they were blessed with three more kids in a rapid succession, and her husband, John had to persuade her to have her tube tide up, with the way she conceived, the couple may be in a competition with the Hispanic group of eight children per couple, John thought humorously, with a liberal ideology which they both developed in America unlike how it was in Africa.

Professor John Solomon Atilogun was in the City of El Paso in the State of Texas for a national conference on immigration policy when he visited along with some of his friends, in the concerts, the Comedy center on Mesa Road downtown El Paso to while away the boring night from a city almost in a desert, after the hectic day of the conference on the impact of immigration policy on economic oil change in the South of America.

One of the comedians on the stage, advised the audience to stay away from Hispanic women if they were not ready to have babies because Hispanic women did not take pills or believe in birth control, the comedian knew he had to be careful with his words as he was just a stone throw from the country of Mexico itself.

As the audience laughed, in his own world John reflected on his own life and that of his wife Marie who kept on conceiving babies and he was glad, he was able to convince her to seal up her tube after four children; he knew he had to work harder, save more, and prepare for the raining day in a country full of tax issues.

What would happen to his wife if something unusual ever happened to him? He thought. He took three-million-dollar life insurance policy with New York Insurance policy Inc., against early death, and that should help in case of anything. He thought.

Sometimes, he wondered why life insurance policy was that important when his Bible told him, life belongs to God who can take or give it at any time.

However, Marie loved to read, and John was happy when she started her MPhil program in Anthropology, in six months, she would be defending her dissertations and she would be able to assist the family, because the student loan she took in the last four years, the cost of books and journals were telling on the family purse, at least by their income in America.

He was the only bread winner of a family of six, and Life in the University environment was a different ball game; association with fellow Lecturers was not as friendly as he thought before he came from Rhode University in South Africa. Race or color was mostly the basis for relationship among instructors, and Professor Bimbo from Nigeria was a good friend, a Professor of Anthropology, a visiting professor to three other Universities in Europe and South America.

Until one day, a common friend of the families of John and Bimbo, Professor Kwame from Ghana in West Africa asked John if he could watch over his son with his family during his two weeks' trip to South America and Ghana West Africa. Kwame's mother had died of old aged, and he had to be there according to the custom to pay his last respect to her in the City of Koforidua in the Northern Region.

John with his wife Marie agreed to watch over the little boy for Kwame for the next two weeks when Kwame would be away because that was the right thing to do for friend's particularly in Plano City in Texas State.

The Couple's apartment had a functional swimming pool, and in the evenings, he would entertain his friends by the pool side while he watched his children swimming. It was how he spent his evenings with any of friends.

The fourth day after Prof. Kwame landed in Africa he called to find out if his son took his medication; the kid was very asthmatic and anemic.

John laughed when Kwame narrated his ordeal about the health problem of his son, he wondered if he should introduce "*Isu meeri*" herbal medication to clear the little boy of any respiratory problem to his friend.

He was no longer listening; he was thinking how the local herb was popular with his mother back in the day in Africa, it was a weekend must for the family.

Any shortness of breath commonly with kids was solved with *"Isu-meeri"* It could make one to vomit and clean the whole trachea of the system of any mucus. It was bitter and could be very irritating or annoying, but it was how his grandfather in village solved almost all the respiratory problems in the village and he gave a warning to all that would use the medication, it must never be sold.

Grandpa believed anything given by nature and Supreme God must never be commercialized, to him *"Isu meeri"* was one of them and John wondered if grandpa knew anything about patents right of products like most pharmaceutical companies in America and all over the world. "Don't worry Kwame he is a bundle of energies" he said.

"And what is he doing now?" Kwame asked.

"You don't understand" he said.

"In fact, he is in the swimming pool with the other children right now."

"Doing what?"

John glanced at the pool at the very spot the little boy was before his telephone rang as if to confirm the energies of the boy with his father, he could not see the kid but he noticed the bubbling water on the last location on the kid, he did not even bother to tell Kwame on the phone what he saw, he was panicking, he did not even inform Prof. Bimbo who was having his glass of wine with him by pool side.

"Oh my God!"

Without thinking or without removing his cloths John jumped into the pool and few minutes after he was not out of the pool himself.

"What is that supposed to mean?" Bimbo asked.

Bimbo felt something was wrong, he too jumped into the pool with the hope of saving his friend and the unfortunate things happened, only Bimbo came out of the water alive but deaf and dump, John Atilogun was drowned and surprisingly, the little boy came out of the pool unscratched as if nothing happened.

It was a sad day in the City of Plano, in the State of Texas, as John got drowned in an attempt save a kid whose spiritual history he was never told before he was placed in the custody of an unsuspecting Professor John Atilogun.

That was three years ago, insurance paid as much as was detailed in the policy after intensive inquiry and Corona report, and Bimbo would remain in a coma for several years to come.

Unfortunately, money could not replace John Atilogu to his family, the kids wept daily as if their father John would come back home from a trip, they were even too young to understand.

Or why would Papa not return home to play with them, to check their homework, and tell them bedside stories about Africa or if he would keep his promise about the whole family trip to Africa as soon as the last born of the family turned ten years.

It was tough and ugly as the happy family house of Professor John Solomon Atilogun became a house of tears and misery. Marie was miserable, she cried every night until her eyeballs were red shot; she lost weight drastically and to the point of hallucinating every night. She soliloquized daily even in the secret of her bedroom, her dreams were like nightmares, she was hunted and most of the nights, she lived on valium sleeping pills to have a sound sleep.

She abandoned the MPhil program at the local University, the children did not believe in going back to school either; they needed their father like a Catholics Priest needed the holy Eucharist communion of Jesus Christ to keep faith with heaven, and it was too tough on them.

The future looked hopeless for Marie, she needed a bigger shoulder to cry on, both friends and unfriendly fellow Lecturers advised her to go back home to Africa with her children, and they wonder if the Continent of Africa was that good like of the immigrants used to say.

They shamelessly reminded her.

It was a mixture of racially condescending feeling towards the misfortune of the family of the late Professor as she was intellectually accenting to the reality of a hopeless future.

The neighbors talked about the families of the John and Bimbo who never recovered from the coma as if they had sinned against the gods or they were visited by witchcrafts from Africa because no such thing could have happened in America, the land of freedom without the secret hands of the enemies, most likely, from their so-called motherland.

If indeed, the enemies were from Africa why did they advise her to go to Africa? Marie thought!

Did Marie go to Africa?

Chapter

2

'Ω'Ω'Ω'Ω

The Oracle listened to Marie as she narrated the story of her life, he looked into her wet eyes for few seconds, he saw a much more troubled woman in spirit than the literary words she expressed, he placed an object like a rubber gun in his mouth, he chewed it like a gun at the same time, he was rendered some audible incantations in a gullible way out of his mouth, it was not gum, it was the balubalu tongue twisting stick he used whenever he wanted to listen more attentively to his clients.

"Do you want to go back to Africa at least for now until there is a clearance from Oluweri," he asked.

"I am worried about everything Oracle, the children particularly my last born Zuno. She is the hardest hit of them all; the Doctor said the tragedy will affect her long-term memory,"

She said in tears.

The Oracle gave Marie a paper towel to mop her wet face and just as she took the paper towel, he noticed her hands were shaking, and he knew if he had to help the innocent lady in the hands of "*Esu laalu*" he must talk to his gods to seek approval.

"It will be okay," he assured.

"Please just tell me what to do. I can't even think straight anymore," she lamented.

Again, tears rolled down her eyes, her nose was wet all over, and she was pulling back the mucus that was almost coming out.

"Relocation is the solution to any misfortune like the death of a spouse. Can you think of a city and job that will take care of you and the children?"

He asked?

"I can't Oracle" she said.

"There are lots of communities of Africans in Austin, and Houston in Texas. You may also wish to consider the opportunities available in those places, any Southern States will be fine to raise the children" He advised.

Marie could still recall a bit of her life before she finally met with the Oracle, she had contacted her prayers partners in the Redeemed Christian Church on Walnut Street in Dallas, they talked of Holy Ghost fire most of the time, and she kept wondering when will the Holy Ghost fire come to ward off the sounding steps of the ghost of her late husband.

Marie could also recall her six months' brief relationship with Ezeolu, from the Igbo tribe in Nigeria; her friends had advised her to consider a faster or early relationship that would take her mind off the misfortune of the loss of her husband. She did, however, it ended in a disaster, she still got a case in court over his death.

Most of the nights, she cried over the death of John her late husband than giving attention to her knew relationship. It was as if the spirit of John was around her most of the time, and it could be true, if not why the footsteps she constantly heard behind her in and secluded environment.

Ezeolu had stayed with her after three months of no intimacy, the evening was great, he went with her to all the places she had wanted to go in the last six months but couldn't because of the misfortune.

She was emotionally getting over some of her depression, for the first time, she started smiling more with a lighter heart, because Ezeolu was funny, he joked over everything, he held her hand like John used to do, and tapping the back of her head and for the first time, when he kissed her, she did not think of John anymore, neither did his face look like that of John, but that of the new man in her life. It was how she realized Ezeolu was a good-looking man

Maybe that will be the end of everything and a new beginning for her, she thought.

In the evening, at home, with just two of them alone, with the kids in their rooms, and sleeping, she cooked the best Africa food he had requested, his favorite pounded Yam with Egusi (Mellon soup) lased with vegetable and smoked fish, which she gladly did. It was tasteful and tonight was going to be the night she would finally give him her ocean of love, the very deep ocean of her love life.

The mere thought of being in his arms alone on her bed drew a smile on her face, she looked at the mirror, the lines of cageyness on her face were no longer there and she was wondered, if it was the new relation or something else.

Hopefully, it will be a breakaway from the commitment she had with her late husband, and it was going to be the final separation from all her miseries.

She thought!

Marie set the table after the children had gone to bed; they were beginning to understand their mother had to move on with her life, her last born Zuno seemed to be recovering from the stress of her late father, just as the reality of the death of their father was apparent to them, that he was never going to come back.

"That would be the best thing for mother."

Mavuso, the eldest child assured his siblings of the happiness for their mother, and they trusted him more than anyone in the world. And when Marie finally introduced Ezeolu to them as her friend, they gave him the respect and acceptance of the trust for a man that may likely bring happiness to their mother and invariably to them.

The relationship with Ezeolu had started slowly and his understanding of her position and that of the children was remarkable, he was a gentleman, he did not take life too seriously, he found jokes and humor in almost everything.

Ezeolu quoted a lot from the motivational speaker late Zig Ziegler of Dallas Texas, Wayne Dyer and Chopra and she could still remember when he told her, what Mr. Zig Ziglar wrote in one of his books that "*Good was the enemy of better things in life*", and Marie wondered if bad was the enemy of worst in life too in view of her misfortune.

Marie had wanted Ezeolu to stay the night with her, from the second week they met, to just to hold her, to tell her if and how beautiful she was, something, she never heard again since John died, it would probably take her mind away from the tears and cries of almost two years and misfortune of her late husband, but she often wondered how the children would feel to find another man in her bedroom, and she was surprised when Mavuso her eldest son raised the issue up about a week ago.

"Mummy, why can't Uncle Ezeolu stay the night with us? We love to hear him tell stories about his village in Africa" she said.

"If you guys will be comfortable with it; I will ask him to stay maybe next week" she told them.
"We want him to stay" they said as if in a chorus.

"What do you guys like about him other than the stories of his village in Africa?"

She asked them, Marie was curious too she wanted to know why they like him or what he said that attracted the kids.

"Mummy, he said he used to help his mother to sell Coconuts in the village Concubine in Imo State in Nigeria and his friends used to tease him and, in most cases, called him Coconut head," Mavuso said, and all of them laughed.

"Did he get mad at them in the village when they called him Coconut head?" she asked.

"No, Mummy, in fact, he turned it into his selling tricks," Mavuso said.

"How?" she asked.

"Uncle Ezeolu placed a written promotion note on his Mummy Shop," she said.

"What did he write on it?" she asked.

"Buy the best Coconuts from Coconut Head" he said.

And they all laughed.

Marie had never laughed like that for a long time, she noticed she could even breathe better now, and she believed the adage that says smiles is the beauty of the face.

"And what happened next?" she asked them.

"Uncle Ezeolu said his sales tripled and his mother was happy," he said.

"I will ask him to stay the night maybe next week if you guys will be happy," she said.

"We are happy already" Mavuso said.

"What about you Mary? "She asked her third child.

"I will like to hear the Coconut Head Story again from him" she said.

They all laughed!

Marie was happy to see the smiles on the faces of her children and she hoped everything would be fine and maybe Ezeolu will provide the missing link in her life and her children.

She prayed.

In the evening, she met Ezeolu at their usual coffee spot in downtown Norma, she kept on looking at him as he talked and held her hand, she did not say anything, and he suddenly asked her.

"Sweetheart, anything on your mind?"

"Why do you ask?"

"You have not been talking much tonight."

"Really?"

"Lay it on me Baby. What is going on?"

"I want you to stay the night with us next Friday after work" she told Ezeolu.

"Will that be okay with the children?" He asked.

"They are in-fact your advocate" she said with a smile on her lips.

"Really?"

"Yes" She answered.

"How?" He asked.

"They put in good recommendation for you" she said still with a thin smile on her lips.

"That is a mischievous smile on your face" He joked.

"What do you mean?" She spoke.

"Just what I have in mind and just wondering what took you so long to do so." He said.

"Your girl is a single mother; I have to be careful" she said. "I can understand." He spoke.

Friday will be the first time Ezeolu would stay overnight with her after six months of no intimacy, between them the evening was great, he went with her to all places she had wanted to go in the last six months but couldn't because of the misfortune.

Marie was emotionally getting over some of her depression, for the first time she started smiling, and started looking at life positively, because Ezeolu was funny, he joked over everything.

What a man! Nothing was ever too serious for him. He held her hand closely like John used to do, again he tapped the back of her head like John used to do and for the first time, when he kissed her passionately other than the lighter kiss on her lips, his tongue combed her mouth, he traced her lips with the tip of his tongue, and she wondered if he took college hours in kissology, or who would kiss a woman in such a beautiful and romantic way?

As soon as she melted into his arms with their mouth together Marie did not think of her late husband John anymore; his face was no longer around her, maybe this new relationship will be the end of everything of her past and a new beginning for her, it would be nice to experience true love again.

She thought!

In the evening, Marie cooked the best Africa food for her man, her African King from Nigeria, he had requested for his favorite pounded Yam with *Egusi* melon soup lased with vegetable and smoked fish, and she gladly obliged him with his local African palm wine and it was tasteful and tonight, it was going to be the night, she would finally give in to the intimacy and it will be a breakaway from the commitment she had with her late husband and it was going to be the final separation from all her miseries.

She thought!

Marie set the table after the children had gone to bed; they were beginning to understand their mother had to move on with her life, as the reality of the death of their father was apparent to them, that he was never going to come back.

"That would be the best thing for our mother" Mavuso the eldest child assured all his siblings, and they trusted him more than anyone in the world, and as young as he was, he was almost fifth teen years old the man in the house to them.

And when Marie finally and formally introduced Ezeolu that a meaningful relationship was about to begin for them and who may be their stepdad in future, they gave him the respect and acceptance of the trust in the man that may bring happiness to their mother and invariably to them. He was no longer just a friend but fiancée to their mother.

Marie went to the Kitchen, after she set the table to get just a bottle of water to complete the table set for dinner for her man, she took the stairs, down to the Kitchen, and just as she took six out of the ten stairs towards the Kitchen, she heard a footstep behind her.

At first, she thought Ezeolu was behind her, men are always in a hurry for everything she thought, but somehow, as the steps got closer to the kitchen without the touch or voice of Ezeolu, she looked around, there was no one, she thought her imagination was playing a trick on her, she moved quickly towards the kitchen.

She turned the knob right and pulled the door of the refrigerator aside, she heard the sound clearly again, it was a familiar movement, it was the same footsteps like her late husband John used to do in his life time, one step at a time, as if he was limping, she felt the goosebumps all over her body, and she knew she was no longer alone in the kitchen, the spirit of John was around again.

Marie looked up to her right, the wall very close to the window, she found the photograph of John she took away from the wall had been clearly hung back on the same spot it was weeks ago, she removed it with the hope of moving on with her life, but with it back on the wall, she was scared.

When she looked the photograph again, it had the smiles of John on it, and it was as if he was communicating a message to her as if to say, I will never leave you.

What did she do?

Chapter

3

'Ω'Ω'Ω'Ω

Ezeolu waited, at the dining table, he felt the food was getting cold, and still Marie did not show up. She had said she was going to get a bottle of water from the Kitchen downstairs, and he was wondering if it were more than just water that kept her for that long, he could still remember how he met her six months ago.

He was attending the Annual Conference of Social Workers in Cleveland in the State of Ohio, when he saw her, she was beautiful, she her lips were full and her set of teeth were tempting, and he eyes glued on her as she walked to the podium to give her talk. He knew he had to know her more than the three days of the Conference.

It was difficult for him to get her attention on the first two days of the conference, it was as if she was evading him deliberately, each time he tried to get closer to her, she would find a way to relocate and she repositioned herself to a reasonable distance from him, until the last day when the conference was almost over, she came directly to him and she spoke.

"I could see you have been looking at me as if you have something in your mind to tell me "She said.

"You got that right. I have and I am still looking at you right now. I am Ezeolu" he said with confidence.

"Marie Solomon Atilogun" she said Solomon was her last median name before she married Atilogun, after the death of John she had started using the name again.

"I was wondering if we could extend this conference to the Starbucks coffee place next door." He spoke.

"Really?" She asked.

"Like seriously" he said.

"You don't need a woman like me in your life with four kids and a very recent widow" she said bluntly.

What a woman? She just laid everything flat on the table for him with those four kids. She was about to move away from him when he held her hand and with all seriousness he could imagine.

"Maybe I could be the big ears to anything you have to say that could make me a better friend to you." He spoke.

"You have the accent from Africa, are you from Nigeria or Ghana?" She asked.

"This question again" he said.

"Lots of people ask you about your accents here in America?" She asked.

"You would not believe it; I answer that question every day in the last seven years"

"That must be tough on you" she said.

"It is my friend" he said.

"Your friend?" She said more like a question.

"Yes, my friend after three days here in Cleveland" he said with a smile which exposed his teeth.

I don't even know all your names" She added.

"I am Ezeolu, the son of Ogbuefi Chiyelugo of Ogbaru Local government in Nigeria" he said.

"What is the meaning of Ogbuefi" she asked.

"It is the traditional title for high Chief among the Ndigbo in the Eastern part of Nigeria" he said.

"What about Chiyelugo?"

"A Chief who gives out cow meat as gift with pride and wealth" he said.

"So, you have enough cow meat to distribute to all your friends?" Marie asked humorously.

"If you were my friend, you would get more than just a cow" he said.

"Really?" She mocked him.

"Absolutely, really" he said.

What a man with confidence? It was quite common with most Nigerians; their men are not like other Africans, when they want something, they go for it.

Marie liked men with confidence, and she could remember all the warning signs they shared in the school about the men from Nigeria, they are too controlling, dominating and may subject their women to something else and most of her friends told her that of the Nigerian men had wives back home in Africa, she must be careful, but this one is different, he seems like a good guy.

She assured herself

That was how it all started, they went for the coffee, and later, to the Movie House and that evening they had dinner together.

Marie had never felt easily comfortable like that in her life with another man for a long time since John died. She told him how her husband died and his friend still in coma in an attempt to save a drowning kid left in care of the family by a friend who travelled to Africa and how his death affected the children and her MPhil Medical Records and to be sincere, she sometimes felt the weight of the misfortune was too much for her but for the sake of her children, she hung in there to dearly life, the life that will change her children and their future.

Ezeolu listened to her, the more she expressed herself, to the point of tears, and the more he wanted to get closer to her, even it was just only to be the pillar of support for her. When she mentioned the three-million-dollar life insurance policy her late Husband left for them, he knew he had to stay with her.

Tonight, will be the night to establish his love for her, and he wondered what was keeping her from coming from the kitchen.

Ezeolu stood up, within few steps from the dining table; he tucked in his shirt and moved towards the kitchen himself. Immediately, he took the first four stairs, he called her name, his voice sounded more like a whisper, he did not want to wake up the kids but there was no response, and everything was quiet and scary now.

Still Ezeolu did not want to keep yelling Marie's name in such a way that it might wake up the children already on the bed. He took additional few steps toward the stairs, and immediately the light in the Kitchen went off.

He groped through the darkness, he reached for the side wall, he could feel the wall and he continued his movement towards the kitchen, his leg felt something on the floor, whatever it was on the floor could pass for a person. He quickly took out his cell phone the light from it was capable of helping him to see his environment even it was a marginal look.

Ezeolu pointed the light on his cell phone on the floor, it was the helpless body of Marie on the floor, he reached for her temple, he could still feel her pulse, he carried her to the living room and just as he was about to press send button for emergence call oh his phone something hit on the side of his head, and he went blanked.

What happened next?

Chapter

4

'Ω'Ω'Ω'Ω

Two months later.

Professor Kwame returned to the United States of America from Ghana after the burial of his mother to witness the most devastating happenings of his life. Mensa his only son; he had left with John his academic colleague had resulted into the death of John Atilogu his friends by the pool side his other friend Bimbo still in a coma.

When the telephone went dead on him, he knew the gods must have dealt a big blow on the Professor, but the fact that his other friend Bimbo a Nigerian was involved meant a different thing to him.

Like the Ashanti tribe in Ghanaians, the Yoruba do not take kindly to untimely death or misfortune like the state of coma of Professor Bimbo, the Yoruba could be fetish to the level of consulting the Shango the god of thunder to find out the reason for the health status of their son and they could come after him.

Kwame dare not explain the circumstance of the birth of Mensa to the families of the late Professor; maybe if he did before his trip to Africa, they could have been saved premature death and medical problem of Bimbos not after the misfortune.

It all started like an unwanted dream, immediately he graduated from the University of Legion in Ghana in the sixties, he met Theresa Kojo his classmate of four years at the college, he was very introverted to the point of disgust, he never had the courage to approach any lady throughout the four years in the University. It was even rumored he was a virgin which was almost true.

As fate would have it, he was in Lagos for a conference and he ran into Theresa, who greeted him with a big smile on her face. He was still bashful, and could still pass for a virgin, not that he had never had a relationship in his life, far from it, but beautiful women always made him uncomfortable, he never wanted to be turned down neither could he look at them directly in the eyes.

"Hi Kwame" she said.

"Hi Teresa, it is being quite a while" he said, not even sure if the sound his voice was his or where did he get the courage, he questioned himself?

"Are you now in Lagos or what?" She spoke.

"Yes, just three months in town"

"If you don't have any plan next week, I am hosting a couple of our mates, and it will be fun to see you there" she said.

"I will be glad" he said.

They exchanged numbers and it was never the same again, by the time he got to her place, it was not what he expected, no one was around, and it was only a dinner for the two of them, he never asked for the rest of the guest, the arrangement suited him.

They talked into the nights, and he was surprised he was at peace with her, and it was the beginning of their relationship. They got married a year after and for five years; the marriage was blessed with everything except the fruit of the womb.

Marriage without children could be a problem in most of the third world nations and it was the case with those from Ghana among the Ashanti people, the woman takes the hard beat more than the man, they would call her names, to the point of disgust.

"Where is my son?"

"He is not in Mama"

"I see, after breast feeding my son for 18 months and if you can come from nowhere to tell him what to do then your days are numbered with my son".

"I can believe you did it for only 18 months and you are complaining"

"Why would you know? You never had a child"

"Mama, I have been breastfeeding your son for five years of our marriage"

"What?" She was mad.

"What about what, Mama?" She said.

"I see the reason why you will never have child for my son"

Teresa was now in tears, what a wicked mother-in-law, did she think of what should make herself conceive?

That was the situation when Kwame came home one night and found his wife crying, she was sobbing profusely and from the look of things, she must have been doing that for hours.

"Baby, what is the problem?" He asked.

Kwame held his wife, he stroked down her temple up to her hairs down to her shoulder, but the tears never stopped, he held her face up, her eyes were red and in pain, whatever was making her unhappy to the point of tears must be too tough for the nerves on her face.

He noticed she had no makeup nothing but just the natural beauty of her dark face and she remained beautiful, even in tears and in pain, it never took her beauty away.

"It is your mother again" she said, after she found her voice.

"What about Mama?" He asked.

"She said she did not know her son was married to a man"

"But why would Mama say that to you?"

"Ask her! I am not God. I can't make baby by myself"

"We have our trust in the Lord. He would give us one very soon" Kwame said.

That night he could not sleep, he remembered how his mother had told him not to marry from Ewe tribe.
"We don't belong to the same clan beside your father was against the relationship before his death, and why you did it is still a clandestine to the family." She spoke

"Mama, I love Nana, she is from a good Christian family, and her father is a Deacon with St Agnes Methodist Cathedral in Accra, give her a chance, she is a good girl Mama" He pleaded. That was five years ago, and the warning signs were all there for him.

Sometimes in his sleep, he would be chased by wild animals, sometimes, imaginary objects would be feeding him with food in his dreams and sometimes, he felt like telling his mother everything, but he knew what she would do, she would just conclude everything to be in hands of the enemies on his father's side and also his wife.

Somehow, the tears of his wife, most of the nights had started affecting the quality of his work also, he was already making unnecessary mistakes at work and it was already affecting his job reviews by his boss, and the Dean of his Faculty was already taking a note of it, however, he felt it will be fine to discuss this issue with his mother. She was the only person he could trust.

The following morning was Saturday, he drove to Afripong Street in Takoradi to see his mother, and as if she knew why he came her words and looks were pregnant with meanings.

"How is he doing?" she said before he could even greet her.

"Who is he, Mama?" He asked ignorantly.

"The man you called a wife in your house" she said.

"Mama"

"Is she a woman? Or how many years more before your eyes are opened." She spoke.

"Mama"

"Don't Mama me with that man you called a wife, I have discussed with your Uncle Kwame in Accra, he would be around to discuss and put some senses into your big head" she said.

"What is my uncle going to do?" Kwame asked.

"He will take you and the man you call your wife to the Shrine of Akwapeng in the City of Latem in the Hill town of Larteh"

That was the situation when he went with his uncle to meet the priest of Akwapeng, but the ritual did not come without warning.

"Your wife will have a son, but you must return to the Shrine with his umbilical cord within seven days after his birth and his life will not be affected by any evil in the forces known to mankind" he said.

"Is that all?" He asked the Priest.

"Yes, except he must not swim in a stagnant water."

That was seven years ago, his wife conceived, and true to the words of the Priest of Akwapeng. They named the boy Asedapeng meaning thank you Akwapeng, his mother was relieved, and he noticed she treated his wife with affection, or why would she not, as she was happy to be called granny like all her friends.

Three years was all it took the family to fall into sadness again, his wife Nhyira had travelled to Koforidua for a conference, and she never returned, no one could lay any hand into what happened, she just disappeared into the thin air, the police and other security agencies could not locate or design why and how she vamoosed.

The frustration and the feeling that she could still be alive was too much on him and his three-year-old son, Asedapeng, in between all these imbroglios and despair, his mother died of Cancer and his life was nothing to write home until he left Ghana for the United States of America after his teaching contract with University of Legion in Accra expired.

In America, he could not even tell the misery of his life to his friends, they just knew him as a single father, as an African in diaspora and they all rallied round him to give him emotional support but none of them knew the spiritual war and ring around the neck of the boy called Asedapeng.

The deaths of his John his friends would have to be connected with his son in the stagnant water as against the wishes of the gods, or how could anyone classify a swimming pool if not stagnant water, he dares not reveal the details of the god's injunctions on him about his son to the families of the two professors, there would hues and cries and they may possibly file a law suit that may in fact end his academic career and possible permanent relocation to Accra in his home country.

He decided to keep everything to himself.

Chapter
5

'Ω'Ω'Ω'Ω

Marie was on intensive care unit of Parkland Hospital in Dallas Texas and when she opened her eyes gently and all she could faintly remember was the food she left on the table before she went into the Kitchen to get water for Ezeolu. She turned her head towards the window in the room; a Nurse was sitting attentively and watching her.

"Where I am?"   She asked. Her voice was more like a whisper. "You are in Parkland Hospital here in Dallas Mrs. Solomon" the Nurse.

"Where are my Children?"

"They are outside waiting to see you."

 "Where is Ezeolu?" She asked.

"The Doctor wants you to rest first" The Nurse said.

"What happened to me?" She asked.

"You had contusion in the head."

She attempted to move her right hand, something held it back, she looked at her arm, it was fully attached to the Intravenous tube, she raised the left hand to her head, and she could feel the thickness of a bandage rapped around her forehead.
"What happened to my head?" She asked.
"That is what the Police would like to ask you?" "Police?" She asked.

"Yes! One of your neighbors called 911 before the ambulance brought you here"
"Ambulance?"

"Yes"

"Where is Ezeolu?" She asked again.

"The Police would discuss with you shortly." She said curtly.

Marie looked at the face of the Nurse with the hope of making out something out of what she said about the Police, 911 and Ezeolu, but none of them made any sense to her.

She watched the Nurse as she rapped the blood pressure calf round her left elbow, she pressed the green button on the Blood Pressure machine, the green light was on and Marie could see everything vividly.

She took her blood pressure on the right arm; it was normal at 127/73 the Oxygen level was at 97 but the pulse was 110 and her blood sugar was normal she checked the IV and marked something on the tube.

Marie noticed the Nurse had a light smile on her lips and probably happy or so.

"When is your shift going to be over?" She asked.

"In the next thirty minutes" She said "

"I did not get your name" Marie asked.

"You never asked me" she said with a smile.

"And how may I address you" "Jenifer "Mrs. Smith" she said.

"I am Marie...." Marie said.

"I know your name already."

She said with a big smile on her face and her beauty just glitters around her face like electricity light on a diamond, what a beautiful set of teeth! Marie wondered if she took a dental cleaning of recent, because they were too good to be natural.

Jenifer Smith thought her shift would soon be over in the next thirty minutes barring any obstacle, the day could be taken as over for her. Sammy, her boyfriend would be waiting outside in the car for her as soon as she stepped out of the Hospital.

Sammy never failed to show up on time, a man who never kept a woman waiting was the way she used to address him and that made him happy.

She considered herself blessed to have such a man, always waiting to do everything right to make her happy, sometimes, she wondered if he was not doing too much for her.

"Please use the call light on the side of the bed if you needed anything" she said.

She excused herself out of the room somehow, Marie did not even remember to thank her; she was lost in her world. How did she end up in the Hospital was still a mystery to her, she closed her eyes, but nothing made any sense to her, nothing at all?

Chapter

6

ΏΏΏΏ

Detective Paul Smith had seen it all, he could sense it when a suspect was lying even miles away, and his instinct were beyond comprehension. He was literarily a short man, about five feet four inches, he had a kind of phobia for tall people, when he was in his teenage years, he took satisfaction in beating up tall guys in his neighborhood.

When he joined the police, he knew it would be the only establishment approved by the system to further express his brutality on the tall guys, this time around; they would not even have to fight him back.

It was his way of getting even with Mother Nature over his height and looking at his family linage, his father had told him his height was from his grandmother and just why nature would place his height in the line of the grandmother he never met when he was born

Paul knew he could now hide under the law, not only to express his anger but to question the nature itself for depriving him the height that could have uplifted his spirit.

Surprisingly, he had the same ugly phobia when his boss gave him the assignment on this African America woman with the death of her boyfriend, he never liked the immigrants from Africa and never stopped wondering why they all keep up coming to the United States of America.

Somehow, there was something unusual about this black lady, yet he could not lay his hand on it, and he knew he may have to put in extra time and attention into how to dig it out, much more than he had in any of his previous cases.

Detective Smith walked into the hospital room quietly like a cat and without taking his eyes off Marie on the hospital bed, he pulled up a chair, he sat down very close to her in case her thick African accent may be too much for him to comprehend, they all do. He did not want to strain his ears to hear her stories.

Not again with these Africans.

"I am Detective Smith of the City of Dallas Police Department."

Marie was quiet; she made no attempt to shake the extended hand to her, she moved her lower lips as if she was squeezing the juice out of it, in truth her throat was dry, and she felt thirsty.

"Another Bitch" Detective Smith thought inwardly.

"Marie, can you recall what happened on the night of January 21st in Eze Olu's apartment" Officer Smith asked.

"You mean in my Apartment?" She corrected.

"Is your apartment on 2172 Skillman Road in Dallas Texas?" He asked quietly.

"No. that is Eze Olu's place" she said.

"Well, that was where we found you" he said.

"Who found me?"

"The Police"

"How can that be? I was in my apartment and was ready for the dinner with Ezeolu, I remember I went to the kitchen and that was all I could remember" she said.
"Umm" he said.

"Where is Ezeolu?" She asked.

"We will come to that later" he said.

"Did you visit Johnson Hardware stores on Forest Lane and Greenville Avenue on Wednesday? He asked.

She closed her eyes for few seconds as if looking for something to help her memory.
"Yes. I did." She spoke.

"Did you ask the clerk to get you the best double edged Madrid knife? He asked.

"I can't remember the brand name, but I bought a knife and a pair of scissors, because I took interest in sewing." she said.

"You took interest in sewing?" He asked sarcastically.
"Yes" she said.

"That sowing interest you had; does it include using double edged Madrid knife?" He asked.
Marie was quiet.

"I can understand that part of a scissors but how will the double edge knife which bought improve your sewing skills?" He asked.

She kept quiet and wondered what and where the questions were leading to. She somehow felt he could not trust this snitch or what else could she call Detective Smith or what did he call himself?
"Where is Ezeolu?" Marie asked.

"Ezeolu is dead" he said flatly, with his eyes fixed on her as if watching for any sign which was exactly what Smith had in mind.
"Dead?" She asked.

"Yes. He was stabbed several times in the head and in one of his eyes" he said.

"But how could he have died?" She said, it was more of a statement than a question.
"That is the reason I am here to find out" He asked.

"He was with me, I cooked, and I went to the kitchen to get a glass of water and that was all I could remember" she said.
"Did you just say you went to your Kitchen?"

"Yes. I was"

"Ezeolu was stabbed several times with the knife you bought with your fingerprints on the handle of it" he said.

Marie's thinking became clearer now; she could sense a murder case was on the table for her, she was afraid.
"What about my children?"

"Your children are outside waiting to see you after this friendly talk."

Friendly talk?

Who calls a murder case investigation a friendly talk than a snitch trying to rope her in? Marie reasoned.

She started crying, Detective Smith was thinking too and as he was thinking amazingly fast, if he was unable to crack this case, he may not get the only Lieutenant position allocated to his department.

He could not afford to fail.

"I will be back after you must have talked to your children, hopefully, you will recall some of the events that led to the death of Ezeolu" he said.

Detective Smith walked out, and just as he was about to reach for the door, he suddenly turned back at Marie, he noticed she tucked in something quickly under her pillow, that sudden movement confirmed his suspicion, Marie knew more than what she told him.

But why would she kill Ezeolu, a complete innocent man or was the death planted? He wondered.

Earlier in his office, Smith had called the insurance agency on the three million dollars' life policy the late

Professor Solomon placed on his life for his family, and everything seems to be fine, with no dirty hands of conspiracy, but why and how Ezeolu got entangled in what resulted into his death would be a challenge for him and his ambition and promotion to Lieutenant?

Whatever she had in her hand which she kept under the pillow must be one of the clues to the mystery on the death of the immigrant from Nigeria.

Outside by the Nursing Station waiting by the door, were the three children of Marie, they looked traumatized, why would they not?

They were just recovering from the death of their father; and now a near death of their mother was very terrifying.

Smith made a call to his office.

"I want you to comb Marie Solomon's Kitchen, everything, fingerprints, even particles of food and time of everything okay" he instructed his assistant.

Smith went straight to the security office of the Hospital on the ground floor.

"I would like to see the video camera room attached to the room 2001 Unit four of the ICU."

"I have no authority to do so, it is against HIPPA."

He flashed his Police barge at the Security Staff.

"Is HIPPA rule against police investigation?"

"No officer"

"And what then is the problem?"

"No problem, you can press the button here for any location you want to see on the screen" he said.

"That is what I thought" he said.

Few minutes later in the control room, Detective Smith was observing Marie and her children in the ICU, and he could hear every word of their conversation vividly.

"What happened to Uncle Ezeolu?"

"We heard he died."

"Is it true?"

The questions from the children were too many for Marie as she cried out in a loud voice.

"Can you all just leave me alone?" she said.

The children could see their mother was in pain, but they needed answers to many questions most of them bother on fear and future of three innocent kids with no physical presence of their father anymore somehow, the Nurse quickly stepped in.

"I think you guys should allow your mother to rest; it is being a long day for her" she said.

It was more like a command than a statement.

Detective Smith watched as both children gave their mother a hug, she gave a longer hug to the eldest son and as if she was whisperings something into his ears, he could see the movement of her lips as if she was passing a message to the boy, it was too inaudible for him to hear anything out of it.

Later, the Nurse led the children out of the room, he watched, whatever was in Marie's tight fisted right hand before was gone. And that further confirmed his suspicious.

Did she just pass something to one of the children? He wondered, he may have to talk the kids, he made for the door as fast as he could. By the time, he reached the ICU Unit, the children were gone. Marie was on the bed with a mischievous smile on her face; her eyes were closed as if she was mocking him.

Smith did not say anything to her, he knew she would deny anything, beside he had no more time to waste, he went back to the Nurse Station.

"Where are they?" he asked.

"Who are they?" the Nurse answered him vaguely.

"The three kids with the Patient in Room 2001 Unit four of the ICU"

"A guy presumably their uncle picked them up"

"Uncle?"

"Yes, that was what they all called him."

"Can you describe him; I mean, the so-called Uncle?" He added.

"Tall, handsome and could be single" she said.

Stupid bitch, all she could think about was the look of the man and whatever was zipped up in his flaps. Smith was thinking aloud.

"Why do you think he is single?" He asked.

"His smiles and his look, you don't see that in married men faces" she said.

"Umm" he said.

"Beside he has no wedding ring on his manicured fingers" she said.

Smith almost threw out; he can never understand women and will never, she even looked at the manicured fingers.

Smith made for the door as quickly as he could, he looked around just as he came out of the building, there was nothing, not even a car movement, everything was silent, and he looked around again and found the security guard by the elevator awfully close to the front door. He flashed him his City of Dallas Police barge.

"Did you see a man with three children in the last five minutes?" He asked.

"A Blue taxicab took them away" he said.

"Did you say Blue Cab?"

"Yes, with a Halloween Sticker on the two side windows" he said.

Can you imagine the difference between a man and the woman talking about manicured fingers if only the world would be filled with men how easy would his job be?

He reasoned?

"Thank you, buddy; he gave the security guy his card

"If you see them again or the cab driver, please give me call" He added,

"I will officer" The security guy said.

"Again, thanks"

"Officer will this improve my resume if my application for police duty scale through?" He asked.

"Anything is better than nothing" he said.

Smith picked up his Cell phone, he dialed the Blue Cab office. James the new General Manager of the company was his boy in the High School and when he got the job six months ago, information gathering process for the police in the city had improved from the oldest and largest taxicab company in the City of Dallas.

It was the general practice for the police to look the other way for unscheduled parking from the taxicab drivers; everything was more like a teamwork. They help to secretly tape suspected conversations in the cab for the police in exchange for the absence of parking tickets for all the company's vehicles in the city.

In this case, both were happy, the profit margin of the company improved, and John was looking good to the investors of the largest Taxicab in the Texas.

PART TWO

Chapter

7

℧℧℧℧

It was a year since James Douglas took the position of District General Manager of Blue Cab drivers in the City of Dallas Texas. At first, he did not like the condition of the company, it had too much of overheads and losses and it was apparent the company without any miracle may go under and it was the reason he was hired to fix things up.

When he ran into Smith his High School Buddy working as a Detective for the City of Dallas, he knew could use him to improve the bottom line and cut down the losses of the company was facing many of them ranging from parking tickets, documentation and too much of paperwork required by the City of Dallas.

James met with Smith in the Blue Club in Downtown Dallas, for a drink and it was the beginning of a working relationship of his company with the City of Dallas and many of the cities in the State of Texas.

Within few months, the company corporate office sent a letter of commendation to him, as the revenue of the company skyrocketed more than seventy percent, losses were almost eliminated and if he continues like that, he could be made the Vice President of the company in charge of the Southern States, and he would be able to buy the property his wife had been on his neck in Livingston Texas by the Lake side.

The request from Detective Smith on the voice message equipment in the most the cabs was against the policy of his company, and he could be fired if the word gets to the corporate that his cooperation with the police was more than just normal.

For James to refuse Smith offer could also be a reduction in cooperation with the police and the parking tickets will automatically be up against the company, that, he could not afford. He had been able to identify the Cab driver Smith wanted to interview and he had reassured Smith that would not be a problem.

"Thanks James" Smith said.

"You are welcome" he said.

Chapter

8

ʹΩΩΩΩ

John Kivis, the undocumented immigrant from Côte d'Ivoire who could speak little English. A father of two and he had left his home country for Senegal when the gold rush problem became the order of the day with many killings and rapes cases, and he feared for the life of his wife and his two daughters.

Somehow, he had considered himself lucky to have the Cab driver job with the Blue Cab organization, but of recent, the management was asking for too much of paperwork that could reveal his true immigration status, by the time he was asked to see the management for an important meeting he knew he would have to quit the job like he did with several others in the last six months.

By the time, Kiwis arrived at the General Managers' office he had made up his mind if he had to leave the country so be it, he was tired of looking and running most of the time because of his immigration status.

However, there was something nice about the James Douglas the new General Manager, he was not the pompous type, he was always the first to say hello to his staff and they liked him.

Even the City police no longer stay on their necks, the parking ticket was almost history and every one of the drivers with the Blue Cab were making more money than what they made under the last management.

It was that encouraging development that made him to accept the invitation to meet with the General Manager; otherwise, he would have disappeared into the thin air like his previous jobs.

"Mr. James would see you shortly Mr. John" it was the Secretary normally call him since she could not pronounce his African name properly, she

John Kivis sat down; his heart was pumping too fast as he asked himself if the General Manager had already called immigration on him what would he do? He thought of his two kids and his wife and how would they survive if he were deported?

He questioned the rationale behind his visit and whatever it was he hoped for the best.

Chapter

9

'Ω'Ω'Ω'Ω

Marie was still at a loss as to how and why John her late husband never suspected any foul play on her part, because he was not the biological father of Mavuso, her first child, and Tide, the last born.

If John did, he never gave her any reason to suspect anything for one moment until his death but surprisingly, he left a will that could only be read on the fifth year after his death that was the specific instruction the attorney conveyed to her two weeks after the death of John. The content of the unread *Will* bothered her

Somehow, John had made provision for his kid's education and generously with a trust fund with Fidelity

Bond Insurance and their upkeeps, pending the reading of the Will that covered all his family investment in gold, and diamond in South Africa.

She had stumbled into some of his investment, and she wondered why he wanted to remain and lecture in the United States of America, however, forty days prior to his death, they both had a conversation on it.

Why can't we go back home? She asked.

"Because it is not yet the time."

"Is it because of the children?"

"It is more than that my dear.'

"Then what it is?"

"When you have finished your program, we can start counting days or months" He assured her.

Prince Oktade Shogun was the guy Marie slept with few days before John surprising came back to Namibia in Africa from a trip that was supposed to last one month, the conference was cancelled or reduced to two weeks as against three weeks he had envisaged.

Prince Oktade Shogun was a cool guy, his biceps and triceps muscle are very tempting to any lady with the spirit of Jezebel, and Marie had plenty of the jezebel in her, but it was somehow suppressed with lots of sermons from her mother.

"Men are after one thing and one only" She repeated all the time and she often wondered if her mother realized what women wanted too out of relationship if not that one thing, she said all the time.

She never listened or never stopped wondering what it was to be with any man solely with freedom to do anything she liked.

Prince Oktade Shogun met her on her way out of the Duluth Hotel after the conference on a developmental program ended Windhoek Namibia. He was exactly what she wanted in a man; he too was all over her like flies to honey. Marie was only 18 years at the time.

"How are you doing" he told her with a stretched hand and as soon as her hand toughed his extended hand, something sent a shiver through her spine, more like touching electric fish.

She looked straight into his eyes and that was all she could remember both were kissing and curling until she woke up on his bed side later in the evening,

When she returned home after the three-day conference it was like forgotten memories and when at the end of the month, she missed her period she knew the father of the baby was never going to be her husband; it must be Prince Oktade Shogun who never called her after the brief encounter.

Marie never stopped wonder how her husband would react if he ever knew the truth about her and the two of her three kids that were not his.

Chapter

10

'Ω'Ω'Ω'Ω

As detective Smith was reviewing all the tapes on the death of Ezeolu in his office, somehow, his mind went to the death of Professor John Atilogu who died with his friend at the pool in an attempt to save a drowning kid, though the case was closed and classified accidental death, somehow, he felt it must be connected with the demise of Ezeolu and the two drowned adults, whatever it was, he could not lay his hand on it, but somehow, he could feel it.

And Detective Smith could still remember all the stories his granny from Cuba told him when he visited her as a kid in Havana. Granny Rocio was not a Christian or Muslim. She worshiped Orisha one of the gods, the slave descendants brought from Africa and some of the stories were so scary, and sometimes he often wondered whether granny Rocio made them up. But why would she? In most of the cases he wondered.

However, he felt the strange deaths of the two professors and how that little boy they tried to save emerged from the water unaffected and if Marie's involvement in the death of Ezeolu had some connections, all these made him to worry a bit more; it was never going to be one of those simple murder cases.
He could feel it.

Detective Smith felt if he had ever wanted to get to the bottom of this strange death, he had to interrogate the Professor from Ghana, the father of the little boy involved in the death of the two professors even if was just to satisfy his curiosity and could feel the solution may even be outside the United States of America if he had to lay the foundation of it at the doorsteps of African stories from his granny.

An hour later on the University Campus staff quarters, Detective Smith was at the door of Professor Kwame, after he knocked three times and he heard no sound and he knocked again, he could hear a movement but it did not sound like that of human, he waited hoping the door would open, it did, what he saw was not what he expected.

The son of the Professor involved in the accident opened the door, Detective Smith to his discomfort found the kid involving the deaths of the egghead of the most prestigious Universities in Texas stood with one leg like a gymnastic acrobat.

Smith felt he must have stumbled into something very unusual in an uncivilized world. He quickly pushed the protective button on his hip to call for back up and somehow within five minutes two other Police cars arrived.

'Where is Professor Kojo?" He asked.

"My Dad went out to the gym for his exercise' he said.

"Do you have his Cell phone number to call him?"

"Yes"

"Call him."

"May I know your name officer?"

"Detective Smith from City of Dallas Police Department"

He noticed the boy talked and sounded like an old man in his fifties, and his left leg which was still glued to the floor was not only white, but it also had marks of a beast on it.

When the boy opened his mouth, he noticed further, he had a splinted and slashing tongue more like alligator. Fear and uncomfortable feeling ran through his spine. He felt he was now on a much more dangerous ground; he reaches for his gun to prevent any attack while he waited with a reasonable social distancing.

For 45 minutes while the waiting game lasted the Professor Kwaku Propeng did not show up Detective Smith had no choice than to take his son to the station.

"Young man I have to take you along. He told the little boy.

"I will not advise you to do that" he said more like a warning.

As he attempted to hold unto the little boy right hand, he felt a sharp blow on his forehead and a kick in the back of his neck.

His eyes went out.

The other two police cars were still outside waiting for Detective Smith to show up when he did not, they broke the door., they found Smith on the floor with no one in site except a black cat which jump out of the window.

Chapter

11

'Ω'Ω'Ω'Ω

Onhanze group in the State of Texas met to discuss the death of Ezeolu and how the family including Igbo community would take the strange death of one of their own.

The last time such a horrible death happened was several decades ago, and most of the present generation could not even imagine the details of the death of one of the most promising sons of Ndigbo.

When the death of Ezeolu was announced in Omunakwo, the whole town wept profusely like kids, and why would they not be touched?

The Head Chief of Omunakwo had instructed the palace messenger to sound the drum in a two for one beat, it was the way the community would normally announce the strange deaths in the land of the seven brave spirits according to the tradition of the people of lower Niger.

What could have been wrong?

They all wondered when the drum sound from the Palace kept on the rhythm in the two for one beat for hours.

The seven leaders representing each of the seven spirits of the community walked in as if their legs were weak, more like they had stiff backs, which could be in truth, as most of them suffered from chronic arthritis, if not, it was assumed old age was common with how they fixed their backs.

Ezeolu from Ogbaru local government came to America on the scholarship from the community and he was expected to return home to head the only secondary school in the village?

However, his death and solution to the cause of it must be managed by the gods, the Oracle of the Hills must be contacted, and his spirit must hunt the killer or killers of the prince and only son Obi of Omunakwo Ogbaru noted for its wars in the primitive era as the seat of all the seven demons in the Eastern Nigeria.

Ogbuefi Ezeolu only son must not die in vain not with all eyes of all the gods opens. It was the way strange deaths were managed in that part of the world from the time Supreme Being Chukwu created them.

All the red capped chiefs and elders gathered by the Shrine of Amadiora, the god of thunder, the priest poured the palm oil libation with Kolanuts on the white three stones already soaked with the redness of palm Oil itself, the judgment must be followed.

The Priest in his white regalia chewed three spicy guinea peppers in his mouth with his countable teeth, with every statement he made; he blew the air out of his mouth as if burning with the anger of the gods, but in fact, and it was the hotness of the spicy guinea pepper hitting his mouth, but who can question the priest in own world.

"I need not tell you why we are all here today" he said.

As he blew the heat of air out of corner of his mouth sideways as if he was smoking cigarette, they all listened with rapt attention.

Again, he grinded his teeth, and tapped the floor with his right leg three times, he then pointed to the bereaved, elder Ogbuefi Ezeolu who sat awfully closed to him.

"This is a fight now between the Onyeocha (Whiteman) our god the unforgivable and revengeful Amadiora" he said.

"Ogbuefi Abaelu who sat very close to the door whispered to Ogbuefi Chiyelugo in a low tune that only the two of them could understand.

"How will Amadiora travel to obodo Onyeocha to fight these Onyeocha gods over a son who took his Islamic offering of saara beyond the mosque?"

"Do you doubt the power of Amadiora?" Ogbuefi Chiyelugo asked in disbelief.

"No, I am not, but wondering if the Amadiora would travel by Air or by sea?"

"It is not our duty to ask" He corrected.

"Which Airline? He asked as if he did not understand what Chiyelugo said. And he could not get any response. He asked.

"Maybe British Airways or Arik Airline.

"Chiyelugo! No gods travel by plane."

"Okay" He agreed.

"We have consulted the gods and in the next few minutes the message may reveal how it all happened."

Within three minutes Okoli walked in with the messages from the gods everyone was quiet, he was not a tall man, he could pass for 4ft 7ins in height, his little mustache and wide nose made him a man to be feared and as if he was calculating the feelings and expectations of the elders, he coughed three times and cleared his throat, just as everyone was quiet, not even a sound.

"What did the god say about Esuedo?"

they all echoed in unity.

"It is not the good news."

"What exactly did the god say?"

"It is not your duty to analyze if it was good or not" Chiyelugo thundered.

"The god said Ezeolu tried to sleep with a woman dedicated to the gods of another land, besides, he was killed by the spirit of her late husband."

"Are you sure of what you said?"

"My elders, have I ever given you any incorrect information from the gods?"

"No, but how can a young man travel to America only to sleep with married woman, it is not only a taboo, it is even an abomination to this land and result it is more than just the late boy alone."

"Please don't pronounce the action of the gods on the family of the Ogbuefi; they are going through a lot now."

"Is that an excuse not to follow the tradition?"

Okechuku asked.

"What then is the tradition on the consequences of the boy's action?" Amalachukwu asked.

"Ogbuefi and his family must leave our community because their son Ezeolu disrespected the gods and the land of our ancestors."

'There must be something else that can be done since the sin did not happen here on Omunakwo land" Ogbuefi Abaelu chipped in.

"The late Prince cannot even be buried in his Village; his family must in secrecy bury him in the forest very far away from the eyes of man, so as not to offend the gods further." Chief Priest Okafor said.

Until this was done, Amadiora cannot be materially appeased, the whole group of elders concluded. After the meeting, Ogbuefi Ezeolu senior was allowed to walk out first as the last respect he will get as the red cap chief after that, his whole family would be declared personal non-grata and must leave the village for seven years in line with the tradition.

Chapter

12

'Ω'Ω'Ω'Ω

The request of the Oracle to Marie was strange; it was straight out of nowhere, in fact, it was more like a shock and renewal of the ugly past all over again.

"What is the name of the boy in the pool when your husband and his friend got drowned?"

Marie closed her eyes for few seconds, the memory and the flashback was very excruciating, a little bang on the left side of her head.

What a question? She thought.

'Akwapeng"

"And where is he now?

"I guess he must be with his dad in Greenville Avenue.

"The name sounded more like the Ashanti tribe in Ghana" he said.

"Yes. From Ghana that was where his father went before the accident" she said almost in tears.

"Can you bring him here?

"Who?"

"The boy that was in the pool before your husband and his friend got drowned?" He asked.

"That will not be a problem" she said.

That was three days ago after Professor Kwame returned from Ghana and a lot had happened, detective Smith had woken up in the hospital after the attack from the Professor and his son. He has not been able to speak, and nothing happened to Akwapeng who welcomed his dad who returned after Smith was knocked on the head.

It was he who called 911 and the ambulance who took the Detective to the Hospital, so far, Detective Smith had remained uncomminuted. He could only smile and shake his head to only one side of his body, whatever it was the reason for his problem, it could not be diagnosed by modern medicine.

It was mission and a treatment the Oracle would have to handle all alone in future.

Did he?

Chapter

13

'Ω'Ω'Ω'Ω

Marie picked up the phone, she looks at the

mouthpiece, it was dirty, and she wondered why her children never cleaned the phone handle when they used, it was not the time to embark on any cleaning exercise, she dialed the number of Professor Kwame, it rang several times and it rolled back to the voice mail box.

That would be first time she would call the Professor after the death of her husband, although, he had called briefly to show his sympathy for her and the children, the second day he picked up his son, after he returned from Ghana and that was it, nothing like a hello or if the welfare of her family mattered again to him and if it will ever go well with Marie or not.

No further communication from the man whose attempt to save the life of his only son resulted in the death of her husband, the father of her four children and action which made her a widow and her children fatherless, it was cruel.

She thought.

It was not the same situation with Professor Kwame; he just did not intentionally pick up the telephone as soon as he saw the name on his caller ID. He could not bear to look at Marie in the eye or hear her shaky voice which contained all her agonies, and to even think his son was responsible was too much to comprehend.

Somehow, he never stopped blaming himself for not being truthful and upfront with the late professor on the spiritual linage of his son with Onyamakoma, who must not be seen swimming in stagnant water and unfortunately a pool could be nothing but stagnant water according to the gods.

Since the Oracle had emphasized categorically on the need to bring Akwapeng, Marie tried the number repeatedly, the third time, just as she was about to give up, she was surprised to hear the voice on the other line.

"This is Kwame and how may I help you please?"

"Prof, this is Mrs. Solomon, and I will be glad if I can discuss with you on Akwapeng later today at the City Library in Downtown." She rushed all her request in one statement before the Professor could design any excuse.

"Six o'clock will be fine with me" he said.

"Me too" She replied.

"How are the kids doing?"

Marie did not bother to say anything; she hung up the telephone on him.

Did she just hang up the phone on him Professor Kwame wondered? And what would she want to discuss with him about his son?

He wondered.

Did she know the spiritual history behind his son's birth? He never discussed it with anyone in America, no matter what was it behind her call, somehow, he too was looking forward to meeting her.

That was three days ago.

Chapter

14

ʹΩʹΩʹΩʹΩ

The City Library closes around 8pm on Fridays except Saturday around 5.30 pm and that will give Marie barely two hours to discuss with Professor Kwame on his son, which was what preoccupied her mind as she alerted from the cab outside the Library in Downtown Dallas, everything around the library had changed and all the cotton around it had been removed it looked cleaner than it was before

Marie walked briskly toward the receptionist who barely looks up, she walked past her, and she went straight to the reference section, to her surprise, Kwame was waiting by the end of the desk.

As she approached him, he stood up, he was thinking, what a waste of beauty and never stopped wondering if she was sleeping with someone else, after the death of her husband but he quickly brushed aside the idea because it was a taboo in his home country Ghana to sleep or date the wife of a late friend not even when his son was partially responsible for his death.

He felt guilty.

"Hello Mrs. Solomon" he said. Kwame extended his hand towards her but somehow, she ignored his warm and moisturized hand.

"Hello Prof?" She spoke.

"You wanted to discuss with me about my son?'

"Yes"

"What about him?"

She took the seat, he pulled out for her with a nod of appreciation with her head.

"I did some checking with a bit of some researches, and it was found out, event around your son birth could better explain how to place a closure to the strange death of my husband and the strange happenings to his friend Professor Bimbo from Nigeria."

"And what did you find out."

"Did you your son have a strange and unusual birth?"

"Ummm" he said,

Professor Kwame's eyes were red and uncomfortable, it was as if she knew all his hidden story as he shifted to the left side of the chair.

"So, the Oracle was right" she said. It was more like a confirmation of statement.

Kwame Kodjo hived, he felt there was no need to hide anything anymore.

"I have never really mentioned this to anyone since I came to the United States of America" he said as if asking for her confidentiality.

"The Oracle would like to hear his story directly from you."

"Oracle?"

"Yes"

Kwame remembered the Oracle like yesterday, he had consulted him in the past, his shrine was too scary for him to follow all his requirement and he had kept his distance but talking and meeting him may now be the solution to the problems he had avoided several years ago.

That will not be a problem, if it will help you."

"Yes, it will."

"Will that be all?"

"In addition, you have to come with Akwapeng your son."

"Will that be all?"

"The Oracle asked for one of his left black shoes."

"Black shoe!"

'Yes Black"

"When can we see him?"

"This Friday if that will be fine with your schedule."

"I can do Saturday."

"Okay, Saturday by 30pm."

"Thank you" Prof. she said.

Within few minutes, she was gone, while he was still thinking of what she said about the left black shoe of his son.

Why will the Oracle need the left foot shoe of his son baffled him?

If that would help, and if it might even lead to the reasons why his wife vamoosed into the thin air, he was prepared to unwrap the misery behind her disappearance, but why just the left black shoe, why not the whole pair or white, just why the Oracle demanded for one leg will remain a mystery to him.

Chapter

15

ʼΩΩΩΩ

Prof Kwame woke up on Saturday morning with a big headache and he had a terrible dream, his son Akwapeng had disappeared just like his mother and the police had told him to accept his disappearance as an act of God, just like the mother.

Immediately, he woke up, he thought he had voices in his son's room, who could he be talking to him? He wondered.

He walked to his room, the little boy was still sleeping, he tiptoed toward the head of the bed for him to look at his face and just he bent down to look at his face, he felt like a powerful hand pushed him aside.

The push could have been from that of a giant, just as he found himself pushed to the floor; he managed to get up only to see his son standing with only one leg with a devilish smile on his face.

"Daddy, you forgot to knock the door" he said more like a warning.
"Ummm. What is all these about?"

Kwame managed to ask his son either out of fear or parental control; however, he kept his distance for fear of being pushed again, not like the evil one who stood with one leg.

"There was nothing to be afraid of Daddy" he said. He lowered his other leg on the floor. And he was back as his son again.

This is about the third time in the last three weeks, he would have to go through this ugly situation, and it was the reason he met with Marie at the Library, he knew as things were if not checked, he may be killed or disappeared like his wife.

"We need help my son" he said. His voice sounded more like a whisper lazed with fear.

"How can you help me, Daddy, I have no control over it when it happens" he said.

"I finally met a man who can help us out two days ago" he said.

"Will he help to find my mother?" he asked.

"That is one of the reasons we have to see him later today."

"Today?"

"Yes, my dear, and everything shall be fine again like when your mother was with us all over again" he said.

Each time he mentioned his wife to his son, he noticed that word alone calmed him down, it could be the only reason, and he has not killed him.

Chapter

16

ΏΏΏΏ

On Saturday, Professor Kwame with his son Akwapeng

arrived with Marie and her first son Mavuso at the shrine of the
Oracle. The waiting room of the Oracle was quiet and primitively
decorated with cowries, and skin of the Tiger and Lion.

Each symbol on the wall had history and they represented the
might of the generation the Oracle wanted preserved in the
foreign land with connection to his ancestors in the Africa.

Akwapeng and Mavuso had never seen themselves since the
tragic death of the Professor John Solomon Atilogun, the ugly
memories of everything came back to Mavuso, as soon as he saw
Akwapeng and what his mother had said about the little boy could

provide her family the closure to the tragic end of their father, he felt that would be fine.

Few minutes later, the Oracle descended from the stairs into his living room and as they were about to stand up for as a mark of respect, he asked them to be seated.

"You are all welcomed to my house"

He directed them to the room on the left side, it was his shrine and most of the stuffs on the wall had no meaning to the visitors, it had meaning only to the Oracle, or why would it be on the wall?

Immediately they sat down, the Oracle looked around and he immediately recognized the Akwapeng out of the two boys.

"Why did you collude with the spirits from South Africa to kill Professor Atilogun and also incapacitated his friend Bimbo?"

Akwapeng immediately took two steps backwards, his eyes changed, and his voice was more like that of a ninety-year-old man.

"Stay away from it" It was more like a command.

The left hand of the Oracle contained the white powered, as he got closer to Akwapeng, he sprinkled the dust on him, and Akwapeng cried aloud like a roaring Lion.

"Stay away from me" He roared again.

Akwapeng eyes were red; his muscles were all too glaring for a boy of his age. Marie was scared, her son Mavuso was crying, as Akwapeng voice filled the room like the roars of a Lion.

Somehow, as the Oracle moved closer to him, Akwapeng dared him, he rushed at the Oracle like a wrestler, but it was how far he could get, he fell and was foaming in the mouth like soapy, wild wind, the spirit in him roared out into the empty bottle the Oracle pointed at him.

" It is over now" The Oracle said

"Really?"

"The bottle would be thrown into a fast-moving river in the down South in the Trinity River after the rituals" he said.

"Thank you, Oracle"

"Don't thank me until you have paid my bills of ten thousand dollars."

It took thirty minutes for Akwapeng to open his eyes, and he had sweat all over his body and by the time he opened his eyes his father could notice his son was different, more alert oriented and just like the son he had always wanted.

Then the Oracle looked at Mavuso as if it were the first time, he saw him, out of nowhere he said.

"The coast to your being king in South Africa will be cleared after the gods in Ghana made peace with that of South Africa and that will be the time for you to ascend your throne."

Mavuso, Marie and the rest of those there were confused? How can a fifteen-year-old Mavuso become a King far away in South Africa.

They all wondered.

However, in two days Professor Kwame Kodjo would have to take his son to Ghana in Africa to remove the final link his son had with demon from South Africa as instructed by the Oracle and the new journey for the fulfilment of Mavuso's destiny as the King would begin.

But how?

Chapter

17

The journey to Kuforidua Ghana to remove the spiritual stone on the side of Volta River to free the soul of the late Professor and removal on the problems on his friend Bimbo was not as easy as expected. Immediately the plane landed in Kotoka Airport, Professor Kwame knew his journey was never going to be problem free.

The immigration was hostile to him, they wanted to know the type of job he was doing to be able to travel to United States of America thrice in a year.

"I teach Anthropology on the traditional African belief, and it involve physical presence in the spiritual needs of the worshipers of Onyankopon"

As he was about to go into full details of the gods in Africa, the immigration officer had already lost interest.

Who teaches scary subjects in the University, he wondered! He stamped his Ghanaian passport and that of his son for arrival.

Onyankopon was not a friendly site to mention, toa n average Ghanaian, it contained many unforgivable and scary stories about this god in Ghana, it was consulted by the Ashanti tribe to fight the white men when they attempted to still the famous Golden Stool, many the whites died strange deaths.

PART THREE

Chapter

18

Marie was born with the spirit of reversed Abiku and one of the ways she could be relieved of sudden death herself was to have three of her husband's die instead.

How the Oracle managed to detect this aspect of her spiritual control was strange, the revelation came as soon as Akwapeng vomited his link to the shrine in Ghana, the small, black, and round pebble rolled toward Marie leg and each time she kicked it away it came back to her.

Who will be number three?

If Prince Ezeolu of Omunakwo in Ogbaru local government of the Eastern Nigeria would be considered one of her spiritual husbands?

"I have no idea of what you just said" Marie asked in fear and with a trembling voice.

"Wait for me" he said

The waiting was for only 15 minutes, and in the backroom within the inner chamber of the Shrine, the Oracle poured the red oil on the smaller shrine by the table stand, with incantations he asked for the gods to open his eyes to solutions for the helpless lady in his shrine.

And somehow, he received what could be called spiritual guidance of how to solve the wretchedness death surrounding Marie, she must receive four incision marks on both cheeks and two at back of her head.

The ones on her face will separate her from spiritual friends and the incision at the back will make them to wish her away from their crowd even if she wanted to be with them.

It was all that was done and that very night after many years she slept well, and it was as if she was separated from something heavier in her that it was before.

Chapter

19

ΩΩΩΩ

Wilson Associates Chamber

When Barrister Wilson sat down in his office and on one of the folders on his table, he immediately noticed one of them was marked urgent, it was the way Tina, his secretary for the past three years normally call his attention to some urgent issues.

On top of it, was the folder of late Professor Solomon who died in a swimming pool about three years ago and he had instructed him never to read his Will contain his disposition until three years after his death and in the next two weeks will be exact three years since the Professor died a strange death in a pool?

The Police report did not implicate his wife, and everything seemed like an act of God and the case had been closed because there was no foul play, the most astonishing part of the Will was the special request from the late Professor, he wanted a DNA test on all his children before his assets in America and tin mine in South Africa could be shared among his family. Brando Wilson reached for the intercom.

"Tina, can you schedule a call on Mrs. Marie Solomon?"

"I tried the number on the file, it was no longer active" Tina said.

"Google her name, social media or 411.com, she must be somewhere" he said.

Few minutes later, Tina gave the Dallas Telephone number of Marie to Wilson. Tina had called her cousin Christopher who worked for AT&T and within three minutes he called her back, she texted Marie Solomon's telephone number, email including Facebook page all which indicated her location was a place in the with the City of Dallas.

Wilson checked the number again, it was a City of Dallas number, he looked at the folder again, he marked the number on the top right of the folder inside front cover.

Did he call her?

Chapter

20

ʹΩΩΩΩ

A week after Marie thought she had recapped her peace with her inner self, the telephone rang three times and before Marie could pick it up, she was tired of everything, the stress and pending murder case of Ezeolu and her daughter who just reached her puberty, she started menstruating.

"Hello" she said into the mouthpiece of the phone.

"Is that you Mrs. Marie Solomon" The Caller said.

"Yes, I am."

"This is Jack from Jack Wilson Associates."

"I hope no one is suing me after all the stress and cases ahead of her. She thought.

"My office would like to schedule a date for the reading of the Final Will and disposition of the estates of your late Husband Professor Solomon Atilogu."

"Will?"

"Yes. Mrs. Solomon Atilogu"

"John never told me; he had a Will."

"Yes: he did, in it, he had instructed our Chamber to read it after three years of his death" he said.

"And what day of the month would that be?"

"In it he said a week after the 3rd anniversary after a Church service."

That will be August 3rd, right?

"Yes"

"The following Monday our office here will send you series of tests to be undertaken by the children before the reading of the Will including a DNA test for the Children" he said.

At the mentioning of DNA test for the Children as required before the will could be read, Marie was quiet.

John was a bastard she thought, he never made her to feel he ever doubted the paternity of any of her children, what kind of a man leaves paternity test as a condition in his Will? She thought

"Are you still there?"

"Yes, I am"

"Good. We have a list of recognized and approved DNA test centers John listed in his instruction to our firm "

He gave you a list. She asked

"Yes, Mrs. Solomon Atilogu. He instructed our firm that any test centers outside those listed will not pass the requirement"

"Okay, I was thinking A & K Laboratory on our block. Would that be, okay? She asked

"Let me check the list first"

"Please do" she said eagerly as if everything depended on it.

"Mrs. Marie Solomon Atilogu A&K Laboratory is not on the approved list by your late Husband"

A&K Laboratory happened to be where Moses worked, an awfully close friend of Professor John Solomon Atilogun from their Universities days in South Africa and Marie had slept with him several times whenever John was away on some of his sabbatical teaching programs in Texas.

Marie knew the first time she had intimacy with Moses was closer to her ovulation period and when she missed her period, she could not doubt who indeed was the father of her girl Dedenda

The 14-year-old girl with her nose and mouth were exactly like that of Moses. She walked like her except for her black complexion everything about the girl was exactly like that of Moses.

Marie somehow found a way to place a strong wedge between her family and that of Moses. In the last 14 years, she had feared what John would say or react if he ever found about the truth.

It was one the secrets she ever kept to herself, however, with the death of her husband she had thought everything would be concealed like a deep ocean in the heart of a woman until this issue of Will in the final disposition of John estate came out.

How would she manage it?

Marie later in the evening placed a call to Moses she was surprised to hear that Moses had died of snake bit after he had recovered from a motor accident, everything around her was happening too fast for her to handle.

Chapter

21

ʼΩΩΩΩ

Prince Oktade Shogun was surprised when the Oracle of the Caves told the elders he, the first born of the late King was not destined to be the King of his people among the Owanbo ethnic group in the Central Africa, but a child he had never seen would be.

The amiable Prince requested further information from the Priest the consequences of being the King in case he defied the counsel of the elders.

What he heard was heartbreaking, six months was all he would rule as a king before his death, and it will be a disaster that will take several years including ten thousand of sacrifices before the tribe could be freed from disobedience from the wishes of the gods.

"Don't do it" He was told by his mother. He was her only son who survived out of the ten children she had for his father.

Some spiritualists have revealed to his mother the witches in the Palace were busy consuming her children until she was taken away after three months of pregnancy to her place in the village of Dankao where she was covered and protected by Obalufon until the Shogun was born, she never returned to the Palace until her son was six years old.

Few years ago, when all the Shogun's three wives could not conceive, his doctor had series of tests done on him and all the results were not all that positive, he suffered low sperm count, meaning, the chances of being a father was very remote.

The Oracle of the Caves was never wrong, and no one had questioned any predictions of the gods in the past that brought their forefathers from the great beyond to the land of Owanbo. That unusual revelation must be a test from the gods.

He wondered.

Shogun had gone back secretly to the Priest for clarification he wanted to know if the Oracle made a mistake or not, but it was very emphatic.

Oracle never made mistakes; he was told. Only his living child, a son he never met would be King over his people, not him. He was told.

However, Prince Shogun could not think of any child he had in the past. He knew he had reckless sex records with women with his people, as a Prince, sex was freely given to him as a mark of respect or what? He could not think of any reason other than that.

And counting the number of women he had slept with was useless, but he could be remarkably close to a figure around several hundred in his forty-five years when he closed his eyes to think of a figure, and one of these women might the mother of the son he never knew. He could not remember who that could be?

How long did he have to go back into his memory lane to search if he had a baby or not? Fifteen or twenty years? He asked the priest. He wanted clarification, at least something re-assuring.

The Priest touched his two eyelids; he pressed them with his thumbs and blew a little breeze into his eyes as if he suffered from eye dusts that must be cleansed.

"Fifteen years" He was told.

Each visitation to the Oracle cost money and libations of six goats and six kegs of palm wine, and secretly, Shogun never stopped wondering when the gods had the time to drink the kegs of palm wine or consumed the goat meat, however, he knew, among the Owanbo, it was a taboo to question the gods.

In the last fifteen years ago, only two women had discussed pregnancy with him, and one of them died three years ago, the other was Marie, who married a Professor from South

Africa and went with him to United States of America, and that was a long time.

Prince Shogun could still recall how he met with Marie, she was barely 18 years, her breast was succulent the size of golf ball and as small as the two breasts were, they were noticeable beyond ordinary in her transparent dress.

She never wore a brazier like most women of her age; her breasts were too small to find her size. Her teeth were small and well arranged; when she smiled, she barely opened her eyes and that made her sexy. She walked like a cat and deliberately stretched the legs like a model in the clothing competition, and her walk could be closer to that of Secretary bird in a Zoo.

"May I know your name?" He asked her.

"Why would you care to know my name?" she said.

"Just hoping we could be friends" he said.

"And what make you think I needed a new friend, or I do not have enough friends?" she asked coldly.

"I could not help it. I like your legs. Are they real?" He said with a mischievous smile on his thin lips.

"If they are not, will that make you unhappy?" she said.

"I will be much more disappointed because they are just too beautiful" He flirted with her.

She took a long look into his eyes, and he too felt the connection.

"I am Prince Shogun and how may I address you, my angel?" he said.

"Marie" she said softly.

"May I touch your leg to be sure they are real"

"You may touch it if that will satisfy your curiosity." She said with a smile on her sexy lips.

Shogun did. His hand contact with her leg was magical, it was warm and fresh, it sent feelings through him like the current of electricity and that was the beginning of the relationship that lasted for three months; it was a very brief romantic twelve weeks, they were together like Siamese twins every night, they walked the park, and he took her on his boat on fishing, it was her first experience on a boat, she was scared, he assured her it would be fine, and gradually she started to trust him, he showed her the trick in fishing too.

"Patience is the keyword my dear, if you really want to get the best fish." He told her.

Shogun held her hand, by the time she looked up, his lips were on hers and as if she too were eager for him, she returned the kiss passionately and like tigers in the jungle, they devoured each other in the dance of the lower hip.

His hand rolled down her underwear and he was all over her, she never resisted his hand when he got her out of the underwear and within seconds, he moved in her, his trust in her was explosive and tearing without pain.

Whatever it was in his hand, had a magical effect on her, and he touched all the most sensitive and electrifying parts of her body, he knew what to do with her nipples, he twisted it, while his left hand never left the inside of her two legs, she craved for him more and more and he went on busting inside her like a Trojan horse and they both climaxed at the same time and it was the best nights for both of them and it continued for three weeks' nights and days.

However, it was one of those things boys of his age did, they never stay too long to avoid any complications; it was how one could get as many girls as possible. He suddenly stopped seeing her.

Just when he was counting his blessing to move to another victim, somehow, Marie with a broken heart approached him two months later that she missed her period. He refused to accept the responsibilities for the pregnancy and whatever she did with the pregnancy or the baby, he had no idea, and it was the last time he saw her.

Later, he heard Marie had married a guy from South Africa and both left for the United States of America. Could that pregnancy be the baby that would inherit the kingdom of his ancestors? And how would he convince her to break her home and marry him as demanded by the gods before their child could be crowned as the King?

"You have to marry the woman for her son to be accepted as the King of Owanbo by the gods"

"What will happen if I found the woman and did not marry her, will my son still be King?"

"You son will die on the day of his coronation, not only that you also will end up in a mental home for the rest of your life"

The search for Marie's address in America became a priority for all and sundry in Owanbo, and it came as easy as the Oracle of Caves had promised and when Shogun asked the Oracle what would happen to the husband of Marie in the United States of America, the gods would take care of it, he was told.
"How? "He asked.

"Never allow that to be your problem, the Oracle of the caves would have taken care of it, just worry about the child, not the husband" The Priest said.
"If that will please the gods" he said.

"And if you must know by the time you will be finding the child, the husband would not be around to challenge you" The Priest said further.

"How?" He asked.

"Leave that to the gods" The Priest said with emphasis.

From the news report he had read Dallas Morning News that two Professors of Medicine got drowned in the pool very close Rockwall Lake in the outskirt of Texas and only one of them survived the other was deaf and dump.

To his surprise, the late Professors was indeed the husband of Marie, whatever he had in doubts of the Oracle and his messages disappeared, it was when he got his travel ticket and book a flight to the City of Dallas in the United States of America.

August 2014

PART FOUR

Chapter

22

ΏΩΩΩΩ

Prince Shogun arrived in the United States of America on an evening flight through Terminal 8 of JFK International Airport in New York on Air Emirates, the immigration process was not as difficult as he thought, because he came with Diplomatic passport, and he was not surprised at immigration officer who was very courteous him.

The flight was even less adventurous than he thought, it was just the regular routine, however, the food on the flight was different than the last time and he never stopped wondering who and how they were able to come up with such a delicious food for such a flight, when the flight attendant asked him if he wanted another plate, he could not refuse.

JFK International Airport had undergone a bit of changes, and much more difficult than the procedure at home which was much more relaxed, and workers treated elders with respect but here in New York they just wanted to do their jobs.

"How long will you be staying in the country?" The immigration officer asked.

"Two weeks" he said.

"Will you be staying in the hotel, or you have a family member or friends to stay with."

"Hotel"

"Name of the Hotel please?"

"Marriott in Dallas Texas"

"Are you here on business or pleasure?"

"Pleasure"

"Enjoy your stay in the land of the Free."

He stamped his Passport, he looked at its ones again before he gave it to him.

Prince Shogun went through the security search and few minutes later, he was out of the door into the sun light outside the Terminal A to connect the next flight to Dallas, the three hours flight to Dallas was just as easy as he could think, and he found himself outside the terminal at DFW Airport.

The Blue Cab Driver was waiting as soon as he came out, the Cab Driver flagged up his name.

"Welcome to Dallas Texas Prince" he said.

"Thank you" he said as he watched the driver who skillfully placed his luggage into the back of the cab. He did not have to worry, as the Cab glided towards the exit road from the North up to the Highway 121 to 635.

Prince Shogun watched the beauty of America, the road and restaurants on both sides of the ten miles' road from the Airport to his hotel, he checked into the Marriott Hotel off 635 Highway on the Preston exit in Dallas Texas.

As soon as he took a shower, he made a call to his contact in Richardson Texas, Justin Adiguka who was a local citizen of Owanbo. He dialed his number repeatedly until the call went to the answering machine, he left a message for to him to meet with him later in the evening to map out their plan on how to find Marie.

Chapter

23

It was three o'clock in the afternoon, the cell room was hot, in the basement of West End Street in downtown Dallas Texas after Marie was re-arrested for the same crime over the death of Ezeolu, this time, however, Marie was worried.

It was all about her life and her kids and it was almost hopeless and for every second in jail, she never stopped wondering if her life would have been better in Africa.

Marie had the same dream again; she was in Africa and there was a celebration of yam festival, each farmer had to display the largest yam tuber in his farm and all the villagers particularly women and children would go round the displayed yam tuber and gave glory to Olodunmare, the Supreme God and in her dreams, she was part of the crowd in Africa.   However, even in her dream, she wondered if she will ever set her feet on American soil again.

Somehow, she heard a sound and most likely footsteps, her eyes were wide open, and later, the door was opened, and it was detective Smith again, with a dry smile on his lips, he was the last person she wanted to see.

"You have been released on bail" Detective Smith said "Ummm" She hummed.

"Don't you want to know who secured your bail?" He asked.

"If you really want to know, I do not care" she said.

"A sponsor and financial of Women organization from Africa did" he said.

"From Africa?"

"Yes"

"Does he have a name?"

"Prince Shogun from South Africa. Does his name

ring a bell?" He asked.

She was quiet for few minutes, as her mind travelled back to Africa, it went down the memory lane, when she was barely eighteen years old and all the young ladies wanted to be Prince Shogun's girlfriend, he was tall and handsome, his smiles alone made her wet and by the time he asked her out she was more than ready. Two weeks after their first date, he asked her for sex, she was more than ready.

However, the relationship had ended in a disaster, it was a secret that had hunted her all her years with John her husband before he died, she suspected he knew everything about her past and probably knew he was not even the father of her first child but he never asked, and each time they make love, she felt a part of him was missing, she could feel it, and why she stayed with her and never betrayed his emotion was a surprise to her.

"You will still be required to make yourself available every Monday from next week" Detective Smith said.

"What did you say?" She asked after she jolted back to

reality.

"We will still require you to show up at the office every Monday "he said.

"I will. Thank you" she said.

"Don't thank me, the case is still open" he said.

Few minutes after she walked out of the Cell, a taxi cab was waiting outside and the driver had her name raised up, he beckoned to her as she moved towards his direction, her mind was wondering, if it could be a plot for kidnap or so, she had seen such in the movies, you come of the jail, and the mafia would be waiting.

"Mrs. Solomon?" He asked her.

"Yes" Marie Solomon she replied.

"I have been directed by Prince Shogun to take you home and other places you would like to go and to schedule a meeting with you next day."

"Ummm and where is the Prince Shogun now?

"Astoria Hotel"

"In Downtown Dallas?" she asked.

'Yes madam"

"Can you take me home" She gave him her address and the Taxicab driver made a U turn to towards the address she gave him.

"How long did you stay with the Police?"

"None of your business" she said.

There was a complete silence after in the car and the Cab Driver never said or asked any other question until he pulled up in front of her apartment ten minutes after.

She did not even thank him; she just walked toward her front door, all she wanted to see were her children.

By the time Marie opened the front door, her children were waiting, they rushed towards her and jumped on her, it was too much for her as she cried and cried very loud and as she was examining each mark on the face of the baby of the family.

Somehow, she heard a cough from the left corner of her living room, she turned in that direction as she noticed a man was sitting in the waiting room and pulling his goatee beard, he was a man she never expected to see again.

Who was the man?

Chapter 24

ΏΩΩΩ

Prince Shogun, never really changed in figure, he was still trimmed set, and he was still with that same mocking smile on his thin lips, his eyes moved like the tongue of a snake and his penciled line mustache was still as sexy as a pimp on the Fountain Avenue on the East New York.

Somehow, Marie could still remember every line of the ugly past and her youthful exuberance in chasing after a man who was the darling of her youth and her generation back in the day in Africa.

"How are you doing Marie?" He said more like a whisper.

"What do you want in my House?" she asked.

"The last time I saw you was almost sixteen years ago," He ignored her question.

"What do you want?" her voice sounded more like a whisper?"

"May I first offer my condolence on the loss of your husband few years ago."

"Umm"

"I read the tragic death in one of our local newspapers and the Palace sent a message to you then."

       Which was a calculated lie, the Palace never mentioned it not even the news media carried it, Marie late husband John, the late Professor of Medicine was not from Owanbo.

Why would his death be news to the people of Owanbo?

"I never received the condolence but thank you, and how is the King?"

"That is one of the reasons I am here. My father died a year ago."

"Sorry about that"

"Thank you."

"And you are the King now or what?"

"I am not?"

"I thought you were the Crown Prince?"

"I was until the Oracle was contacted."

"Oracle?"

"Yes. Oracle of the Caves and Hills"

"What was the business of the Oracle in it?

"No king is ever crowned without the confirmation and approval of the Oracle of the Caves and hills."

"Can you just sit down?"

'Thank you."

Prince looked steadily for few seconds into her eyes; it was one of his sex appeals to women. No matter their reluctance, a mere looking in his eyes into theirs was all it takes for them to melt, they always do. He was sure of himself.

"Ummm. I have come to re-write history."

"Re-write history?"

"Yes"

"With whom?"

"With you"

"On what?"

"To press for a reset button, down the memory lane."

"Of what?"

"Few days ago, I sent one of my boys to the school of your son, his DNA sample was picked up as the direct blood of Owanbo. And it is time for him to fulfill his role to his community in Owanbo."

"My son is an American?" Marie said with a lower voice.

"I am aware of that; he is also from Owanbo."

Shogun had expected Marie to dispute the DNA story because he never really checked the DNA of her son, it was a gamble on his part to alley his fears if he was dealing with the wrong child.

"And how have you been doing with the four kids?" Prince Shogun said as if he was trying to change the topic.

"Have you been counting my kids or what?"

"Nothing is hidden anymore these days" he said

"We are doing fine with the support of the community and until the death of my husband and his friend Bimbo from Nigeria" she said.

"I have come to take you back home."

"My home is here in America, besides my Kids are too young to live in a country without electricity and their regular McDonald breakfast."

"I can bring **McDonald** franchise to Owanbo if that will make you happy."

"No way"

"And **KFC**"

"No thank you"

"I can add **Chick Filay**" to it if that will make you smile"

"It is still no, even if you bring Wendy's to Africa" she said as if mocking his assumed authority to attract any franchise deal to Africa.

'Would you care to show me your city tomorrow and we can discuss more on the future of our son" And he stood up and if he were about to go.

Marie suddenly realized the Prince Shogun was the only friend she had after he bailed her out of the police custody and the case in court over the death of her boyfriend and she must learn to trust somebody again.

"I am a little tired now, I have to shower and rest for the night, you may give me a call tomorrow" she said.

"I will "

"Thank you for bailing me out "she said.

'You are welcome." He said with his mischievous trademark smile,

PART FIVE

Chapter
25

Elders of Owanbo

Chief Silki Teko could not have been more than sixty-five years old, he had a funny way of laughing to the left side of his mouth, a bald individual, he was one of the most difficult elders out of the Kingmakers of Owanbo Clan

He never looked at any issues objectively, he was in the class of the people that would first consider things negatively before they could be made to see the positive side of anything in life and in most cases, it even takes a longer time to convince him.

Chief Teco Silki walked into the palace with a nostalgia look, the palace was empty now and it was too silence for him, the late king was a nice friend of his, and he was happy when the Oracle denied his son Prince Shogun the throne.

Why?

He never liked Prince Shogun, the only surviving son of the late King, he considered him too arrogant and a cheat with most of the women, he deflowered with his adulthood.

How could he forgive Shogun the Prince he did to this daughter, he thought his daughter was happy with the prince and he was already looking at himself as the in-law to the King through the Prince, which would have improved his status within the Kingdom, until the younger Prince broke his daughter's heart emotionally, the poor girl never recovered from it.

Teco Silko was happy after the revelation and the denial of Shogun as the King of Owanbo by the Oracle, he made it his duty to get closer to the priest of the Oracle of the Caves to add more to the problems of the prince.

"The prince must cross all huddles" he told the Priest after he had laid down his gift to the priest of the Oracle of the Caves.

"He will, unless he wants the right to the throne taken from his family" The Priest emphasized.

And when this is over, I will see you with more of what can make the gods happy?

And will that be? The Priest asked.

"One acre of Kolanuts farmland" he said.

"Make it two, my friend for the gods to be very happy" He chipped in.

Both smiled, no handshaking was taken, In Owanbo clan only words and a straight look into the eye in front of the gods were considered enough. And whoever go back on the agreement would always be visited by the gods.

In the Oral history of the people of Owanbo about two hundred years ago there was the story of man away from his words and ended in a mental hospital after he went back on his promise in the presence of the gods.

Chapter

26

Reconciliation with the gods in Ghana

"You will have to go to Ghana with the Professor" the Oracle said after he had made ritual consultations with the gods and that was a surprise to Marie.

"Why Ghana?" She spoke.

"Because it was the only way to end the mystery surrounding the problem."

"Prince Shogun of Owanbo came last night Oracle" she said.

After a brief history of what happened and the arrival of Prince Shogun, she was surprised when the Oracle looked at her in the eyes and said Prince Shogun would have to go with her to Ghana to complete the ritual associated with the gods in Ghana.

" Supposed he refused?" She asked.

"He will not, unless all he came for, from the land of Owanbo in Namibia would end in vain" Oracle accentuated.

As she was about to leave, the Oracle asked her if she had gotten intimate with the prince since he came back into the picture.

"No" she said.

"Don't until the outcome of your trip to Ghana is known." He warned.

"Is there any reason for it?" She asked,

"The gods would not be happy if you do, until all obstacles are removed."

When Marie arrived home with her son, she was surprised Prince Shogun was already waiting for her. His rented black Mercedes Benz car was parked outside.

"How did it go?" he said.

"Not as planned" she said.

"How?"

Did you not ask me to show the city last night?

She mockingly said.

"Is that a yes or what?" he said.

"Give me 30 minutes to dress up". She left him sitting at the living room.

One thing was clear Prince Shogun was particularly good with the kids, he hits it with the Marie four Children right away including his own son who has not been told the task ahead or if he was indeed his father or not, all they were told was a Prince of Africa was their guest.

Thirty minutes exactly Marie appeared in a black evening dress good enough for a dinner but not too tempting for the eyes of Prince Shogun, with just little instructions to the kids to keep the house safe, Marie went out with Prince Shogun.

What happened?

Whistling at night

Can attract

evil spirits and ghosts

Chapter 27

The Akan ethnic group back to Trip to Ghana

By the time, the Professor Kweku, his son, Marie, her son and Prince Shogun arrived at DFW Airport in Dallas Texas it was never a surprise to them all that Prince Shogun had paid for the trip.

To the Prince, the cost of the trip was indeed part of his atonement for the sins of the past as requested by the gods, every bill associated with the trip must be paid if he indeed wanted the gods to smile at him, it was how the Priest for the for the Oracle of the caves had instructed before he left Africa.

In actual fact, the gods had nothing to do with the cost or payment, it was part of the deal with Chief Teco Silko, one of the leaders of the community who had connived with the priest to have Prince Shogun punished for abandoning his daughter even if it means paying more for everything that will prevent him from becoming the King among the tribe of Owanbo in Namibia.

Welcome to Kotoka International Airport was the big sign they saw as the plane landed in West Africa, a first trip to Ghana for most of them except Professor Kwame, after the long 10-hour direct flight connected from DWF to Atlanta and looking at the moderately beautiful Airport in the heart of West Africa, it serves Accra the capital of the nation of Ghana in the West Africa.

Kotoka International Airport operation could be by the Ghana Airports Company, and it can be taken as the sole International Airport in Ghana. The story behind this beautiful pride of Ghana could be traced to her colonial history with the United Kingdom, it was originally built by the British Royal Air force during the second World war which ended in 1945.

In 1956, a year before Ghana attained her independence from the United Kingdom, it was handed over to a development authority and by 1957 when the country fully independent it became the Airport, and as small and moderate as it may be. it became the pride of the new nation in West Africa, and it could be taken as the first Airport fully owned by any independent African country in 1957 and why would it not?

Other nations in West Africa including Nigeria were not ready for their independence from the British, most of them were busy doing something else until Ghana took off like a rocket and it was then most of them stepped up their demand to be independent nations.

By February 1966 in West Africa, a month after the first Military coup led by Major Kaduna Nzeogwu, in Nigeria on January 15th, 1966, had killed Alhaji Tafawa Balewa the Prime Minister of Nigeria and some others, Ghana a neighboring country in West Africa like Nigeria had her own military coup and the first President of Ghana Osagiofor Kwame Nkrumah who had turned the British leftover of the air force base to International Airport was removed.

A year later a member of the military National Liberation Council Major General Emmanuel Kwesi Kotoka General Kotoka was killed in a place not too far from the Airport and to the surprise of all, the then military government in Ghana renamed the Airport after General Kotoka with a big statue of his for visitors.

As the economics of Ghana which had taken a downturn in the eighties and nineties continue to improve with good systems in place, Kotoka International Airport became the Hub for Africa business with almost 3.7 million visitors' yearly and by 2020, it was an indeed a bad year for most of the Airports worldwide because of Covid19 and it took a big hit on Kotoka International Airport and its passengers level dropped to 1.8 million.

The immigration process was not as difficult as they had thought of the new regulation from African Union did the magic, no black man must be subjected to any immigration hardship in any African country, ones in Africa, every black man must be seen as returning home to his motherland, the homestead of their ancestors, it was the policy most African countries had adopted to welcome the blacks all over the world taken away by years of slavery.

To find the best hotel to stay in Accra was not difficult, all had been arranged by Prince Shogun's protocol officer from Namibia and within two hours in Accra they were all in their hotel rooms in Marriot's Hotel.

Within hours of arrival and special treatment from the Airport to the hotel and special food and attention on the flight, Marie was wondering what other surprises the trip would offer and despite the warning of the Oracle for her not to have any intimacy with Prince Shogun, she was already fighting against the temptation.

After the breakfast, in the following morning, after their first night in Ghana, they would have to go by road on a four-hour trip to the village of Akran to meet with the Priest of Odomankoma and Onyema among the Akran people next day as arranged.

Overnight, Prince Shogun had thought over everything, maybe he will finally ascend the throne of his ancestors, things are working according to the plan, and he started having feelings for Marie and was hoping on what a future with her will offer him.

Despite Marie's' four children she was still beautiful with those hidden smiles and beautiful legs of hers, more than three times, on the flight, he had looked at her legs when she left for the bathroom on the flight, he had wanted to go with her or do something to show he care, and he was thinking how the last 17 years had been without her and where to pick up the relationship if there is any sign of it in her.

When she took him out to see the be City of Dallas, and the new roads they called High five Highways between 636/75 almost opposite Texas instrument, he wondered if he could ever turn his city in Africa around to be as beautiful and as nicer place like Dallas Texas. Marie was not asking questions as if she wanted the answer back and how it could happen depends on her, at the same time, he noticed something was holding her back from physically showing her true feelings for him, as if she still had a place in him in her life again.

Somewhere, in Dallas Texas in the United States of America on Greenville Avenue almost closed to Mockingbird Avenue was Papandreou eating place with lots of beautiful restaurants was where she had taken him.

After tasting one or two sips of the soup and a big bite of the meal, he knew why she did it and It was the best meal he ever had he had been visiting America and he could now believe the slogan that everything was big in Texas, the beef was soft and delicious, the whole meal was like party food with special attention to details, the environment was like a Buffet.

When they stood up to go his hand had deliberately brushed hers and he felt the succulence of her skin and a form of electric shock travelled down his spines. Could he be falling for her, or it was just the tipsy wine he had?

He reached fully for her, she never stopped him, nor did she encourage him. He held her and when he attempted to kiss her, she stopped him

"Not now" she said more like a whisper.

He noticed her eyes were fixed on him; he could see a bit of a tear gland at the edge of her left eye. Did she cry overnight, or his eyes were just messing with his imagination? Her body were moderately warm, his mouth and hers were about two inches apart, and he respected her words when she said not now.

Now with her in Africa in Ghana things would work out well he hoped.

Chapter

28

Marie in her room, in the hotel had thought about everything in her life in the last two weeks since Prince Shogun arrived Dallas to bail her out of the murder case the sneaky Police was almost wrapping on her until her savior Prince Shogun arrived the scene, what it was or what he did the charges were dropped and she was even cleared to travel out of the country or how could she have been allowed to leave the country with a murder case around his or her neck but it did happen.

The Family of Ezeolu from Nigeria had even written the Court they were no longer interested in pressing charges against her, somewhere, it was like the gods in the South of Nigeria among the Igbo had decided to allow the sleeping dog of the late son of the soil Ezeolu to sleep to eternity.

Her children too slept well, the younger one with nightmares, never show any sign of it again, whatever it was, Prince Shogun presence must have brought peace to her from

Africa, which had eluded her since the death of her husband by the pool in attempt to save a drowning kid about three years ago.

Just when she was thinking her life would be positive and stress free again and as she was looking at a positive future with the Prince, the Oracle had instructed her to avoid any intimacy with the prince until the whole problem was over.

Which problem again? She wondered.

It was not how she felt inside, the fire inside her to give herself to him when he almost kissed her, the feeling was too much, and she could have given herself to him and right now she wondered why in the hell she did not ignore her very weak "Not now" warning.

To her surprise, the prince obliged her request to stop, she too almost blamed herself for uttering the word out at all, her legs were weak with feelings for him, her lower lips were opened and ready, and if he had attempted to kiss her after her first refusal, the warning signs or instruction from the Oracle would have been ignored, she would probably have ended on his bed.

Whatever the Oracle found as the reason to deny her the intimacy must be exhumed in Ghana, and she must learn to be patient, from everything she knew and heard that Oracle was never wrong.

And she wished the Oracle could be wrong at this time around, at least one time, for the sake of the fire in her body.

What happened in Ghana?

An itchy foot means

a long

journey is likely

Chapter

29

The trip to clear with the gods.

When it comes to African religions, most of them do not have sacred tests, but symbolic language and written symbols and it was the same in the Ghana among the worshippers of Akran religion. It uses symbols created by the Ashanti craftsmen, the word Adrinka among the Akran was an indication for the way of life of the Supreme Being and it was called Onyema.

When Prince Shogun read and researched into the gods in Ghana, what he found amazed him unlike what was operated in his country in Namibia. He could not understand why the god called Odomankoma was a short-lived Ashanti creator, even though it was assumed as to be Supreme God to everything, but sadly, death put the so-called supreme God out of business and was replaced by Onyema and Onyankopon in the Odomankoma, meaning a god responsible for both natural and supernatural existence and could be taken as the architect or maker of nature.

The scheduled visit to the Priest of the Odomankoma shrine was arrange by the Professor from Ghana, he had arranged for a car to take all of them from the Hotel to the shrine.

The little Stola village few miles away from Takoradi and Accra it was not as fanciful as anyone would imagine; the roads to it were narrow and dirty, not even a streetlight and it was as if the roads never saw cars for months, or generation and nothing much more could be of interest throughout the 45 minutes trip.

However, as soon as the cars stopped by the priest house, no one within the entourage could question the ownership of the only structure with minimum resemblance to civilization in the whole village.

What happened in the shrine?

PART SIX

Chapter

30

Trip back to USA

It has been a stress-free trip as mentioned by the Oracle, from Kotoka International Airport to the gods of the Odomankoma, in the village of Stola, they have all walked round the Stola Stone seven times as demanded by the priest of Odomankoma, they picked a table spoon of the sand around it and the priest had used it to appease the gods and they were free from the curses that could have led to the several deaths, at least that was what they were told.

With assurance that the peace and had been restored to the all the families involved and communication established with the gods in Nigeria over the death of Ezeolu, and that of the Owanbo tribes in Namibia over the right to the throne of the tribe which was the reason Prince Shogun had come, however, only one thing was not solved everything including the next steps must be cleared with Oracle in Dallas, in Texas in the United States of America which will provide the closure to all the problems.

The night before the trip back to United States of America Marie had been relieved of every anxiety, with the outcome and the acceptances of the sacrifices from the gods, she wanted to show a bit of appreciation to Prince Shogun for his kindness and financial support in the last one month and how the City of Dallas Chief of Police and District Attorney had written to her that the murder case had been dropped.

Both had gone out into the beautiful City of Accra for the night, they walked by the roadside like regular local people of the Fanti tribe, they bought Suya by the roadside and were free from all the regulations of United States of America, it was the most exciting moment of Marie's life since John died, the prince eyes never left her face for a second and both could feel the chemistry of it as if it was right for everything.

By the time they returned to the hotel, it was obvious of what to expect, when Prince Shogun kissed her by the lips, her lips and legs were too weak and ready to refuse him, she too returned his kiss like the coils of a snake around Iroko tree, his tongue was warm and demanding and hers was responding and eager for his and they were all over each other like anything anyone could Imagine.

Unfortunately, none of them remembered the warnings signs from the Oracle never to have any type of intimacy until they returned to United States of America with a teaspoon of the sand taken from Stola shrine in Ghana.

Unknown to them, the sand and application of it with others stuffs by the Trinity River in Dallas Texas was to be the complete separation from the spirits of her late husband for her and the curses that planned to kill three of her husband and lovers because she fell from the back of her mother as a kid in Africa.

Marie made love to Prince Shogun like a hungry tigress, she was all over him and he too went with all her drives, the prince in his own way and moves rejuvenated Marie back to the first time they first met, the level of ecstasy was more of forgiveness of the past with a complete movement into the future. She remembered the second Shogun slept with her after several years, she ran into him at a conference ad before anyone could say Jack Robinson, they mad love and she could not be surprise as to the paternity of her daughter when she was born nine months after.

Whatever the Oracle had in mind about abstaining from one another had no meaning to both, of them, the gods to them must be wrong. When Marie stood up to go into the bathroom, Prince Shogun took another look at her, he realized how much he loved her and wondered why he never made amendment or kept her to himself in Namibia all these years.

What was it she said about the Oracle in Dallas about intimacy with him? Who cares! He wondered the so-called Oracle never knew about Okafor's theory in his younger days on relationship, maybe the Oracle was overrated or why would any Priest of the gods use some unscientific method to prevent true love she wondered

The theory had never been proved wrong. It stated that in any relationship with any woman you have had carnal knowledge with it should never be difficult to reestablish carnal relationship with again.

Chapter

31

A day before the Will

It was the second week of August after Marie and Prince Shogun had returned from Ghana, it was the way the journey was predicted by the Oracle, without any stress, the gods in Ghana had taken all supplements of ritual as demanded and Marie with her four kids were looking forward to a new life as promised by a much more loving and gentler Prince Shogun.

Marie had given the small teaspoon of sands from Ghana to the Oracle, unfortunately, to her surprise; the Oracle had asked if it was the same sand from Stola Shrine and she had confirmed it to be so, still the Oracle asked again if she was sure or not.

Whatever, the result of everything will be done solely by the Oracle by the Trinity River in Dallas?

The post office package as received a day previous was from the Law firm of Jack Wilson Associates; on the front of the packed it says *the final disposition of John Will.*

Marie had taken her four children for the DNA paternity test as requested by the Law firm before she left for Ghana, the result of it would be read on the day of deposition says the information in the package.

The neatly addressed and wrapped package contained a covering letter which detailed the meeting place and who would attend. Marie was not expecting more than herself and her four Children in attendance, for her, not to be alone she had requested Prince Shogun to accompany her.

Instead of the limited number of people she had envisaged, the crowd waiting was more than 100 people including the Local television.

Why?

John her late husband belonged to many societies in the state of Texas and in his home country in South Africa among the Zulu and all of them were in attendance.

Unknown to many of them, including Marie, John came from a mining resource rich family in South Africa and he never for one day hinted to his wife how rich and what was on the table for her in term of inheritance. He was seen more from the academic standing than the wealth of his family.

All the years of his marriage, he never exposed his wife to his place of birth and the deeper sources of the financial empire willed to him by his grandfather the Oluwajin of Zululand. It would be day everything about the late Professor of Anthropology would be known including the children from the undisclosed for relationship.

How did it go?

Chapter

32

Disposition

The reading final Will of John came with many surprises as could be expected, the opening was not without prayers, and it was led by a traditional Priest from Swaziland. He called on the gods of Africa to display law and order with the controlled strength.

Shango the god of thunder was noted for with all his authorities and with that, orderliness took place because the god of Thunder was in attendance according to the belief of all the attendees.

The things on the list were the items given to the family and everyone was happy with what they got until the Court clerk brought out the DNA Report as the next item on the agenda. Marie was not happy; it was not what she thought would happen and why would the DNA report be read in the public. She now hated John sincerely, because all her hidden ocean of misery will be known to the public

The Magistrate read each name of the children one after the other and related their DNA result to that of John, the result was astonishing, the paternity test result proved that out of the four children only the second child of Marie was late John Solomon Atilogu's son, others were not.

The second son Manish would be the only child to inherit everything from the mining industry and two commercial banks in South Africa with nothing for others including Marie herself.

In the last paragraph of the Will John had written and poured out his pain in all the years of his marriage because he knew and suspected the children were not really his, he detailed how he felt one of his best friends Moses of the AK Laboratory slept with his wife, he described his wife as the must mischievous one with no respect for their matrimonial home.

The final outcome was damaging as everyone walked out on Marie with shame, all her friends, and even adversaries within the family made uncomplimentary statement on her, only her children and Prince Shogun stayed behind. It was even pathetic as the two children denied in the disposition wanted to know who their father or fathers were.

Chapter

33

The Owanbo ethnic group back to South Africa

The outcome of the Will disposition of John was very devastating to Marie; however, Prince Shogun was indeed the winner in the whole problems of Marie. Instead of a son he came for as his, he had two from the four children of Marie, he had children.

The first son whose name was Mavuso, and the third child of Marie a girl whose name was Denide by now he asked himself, if he had to get used to seeing himself as the father of two instead of one.

What was even the name of the girl? He asked himself; he could never stop wondering how the girl was his after a brief encounter with Marie in the hotel during his visit to United States of America after several years.

And as happy as he was. He could not fully remember how the third child of Marie was his except when he was in the United States for a conference, and he had run into her and it was a brief encounter in his hotel room and could not believe it turned out the girl he never had.

Mavuso the first child of Marie looked exactly like him, he had the big nose of his father and the mouth of his mother, his gaits were exactly like his own and he had no doubt, Mavuso would win the hearts of his people at home in Namibia.

With the disposition on the paternity of her children in a public domain, she could remember who was actually the father of her daughter, it was Prince Shogun.

Chapter

34

The flight to Namibia took off from DFW International Airport in Dallas Texas on time, it was not a direct flight to Hosea Kutako International Airport to the land of the brave in Namibia as the they were called, the first stop over was Heathrow International Airport in United Kingdom.

It was a first-class reservation, Marie did the reservation herself including the children, she never stopped wondering if she were going to wake up to find all her so called happiness would just be a pipe dream, but was indeed real and clear, a perfect home coming to the land she never thought she could ever returned not just that she would be mother of a young king with lots of responsibilities among the people who would love her and respect her unlike the United States of America where every Blackman is still being chased with the history of slavery despite two centuries.

Marie had a terrible dream; in it she saw a Cobra neck of with almost the length of six feet chasing her and when she woke up the flight was going through a turbulent glide in the sky the Pilot was asking all of them on board to check their seat belt. It must be a dream she thought unknown to her, it would be one of the prices she may have to pay because she defied the Oracle instructions on her trip to Ghana

She had been warned never to have any sexual encounter with anyone particularly Prince Shogun before the ritual must have been completed, it was supposed to be a complete separation from the spiritual attachment of the gods in Ghana with that of the gods Namibia for her to have a blissful life after.

Marie had defied the Oracle, she slept with Prince Shogun not just one time which the gods would have taken as an accident of the flesh, she did it several times as if she gave the middle finger to the gods or the Oracle himself for his messages, and nobody ever crossed the messages of the Oracle without repercussion.

What happened to Marie after?

Chapter

35

CORONATION

The crowning of Mavuso as the new Owanbo King was expected, it was predicted by the gods that his father Prince Shogun would not be King of Owanbo due to many reasons including a spiritual woman he slept with in the past which had taken his honor and glory away from his destiny, only that woman could restore his glory through the fruit of her womb

The young Prince upon arrival with his father in Namibia had created a relief and his presence a joy to the people of Owanbo been taken into a secluded custody to dine and wine with the gods, the rituals towards the crowning was scaring, the preserved tongue of the previous King must be eaten by the prince as a symbolic transfer of the spiritual power and authority from the past to the present. It will not be the first time; it was a custom laid down by the gods for Ovambo people for thousands of years.

Later in the night, Mavuso was taken to all the corners of the Kingdom at an unusual hour of the night, in the company of the seven witches of the Kingdom, they were considered the guiding forces for the people particularly in the night when all forces unknown to regular people walked around.

All the seven women had passed their prime in age and in appearance, whatever they look like, they were not the kind of faces you wish to run into in the daytime, almost everyone of them had no teeth, two of them had deformed back, one was blind and the other four were very short and they walked as if they had infections or chronic arthritis.

The Chief Priest who was chanting some spiritual incantations handed the sixteen-year-old prince to the old women and retreated to his shrine. It was a taboo to ask or question the women what they planned to do with Prince or where they were going.

Will they bring the young Prince back alive? Or he would be used as sacrifice in the spiritual world? That was the question from all and sundry, in the history of Owanbo, only one time was a selected prince for the Crown was taken away and never returned, and no one asked any question, it was like it never happened and they moved on.

However, with Mavuso as their new King, the elders were trilled for all the events that led to the installation of the new King, the youngest in the history of the tribe of Owanbo went well, throughout the events, nothing unusual happened, the rain was very light, the sun was moderate even the wind accepted the events as defined.

The climax of everything was when the new King was expected to select one of the three bowls of calabashes in front of the Palace in the presence of all, the outcome of his selection would indicate what his reign would be for the people.

The first calabash was filled with honey, a selection of it would indicate his period would be glorious or what else could taste better in the mouth than honey? It was the chief priest himself who had gone into the forest to get the undiluted honey from the top of Iroko tree, it was not clear how he climbed the 40 feet tall tree, but he did within ten minutes, and he was back.

The second calabash was filled with water given to the Palace with the approval of the river goddess of Ehimirin, meaning, if the king ever selected this calabash with water, his period will forever be seen as a time of plenty for the people and the farmers in particular would have enough rains for favorable harvest, and the weather would be favorable to all, water was never the enemy of the people, at least, it was the belief of the people of Owanbo.

The third calabash was filled with spicey tatase pepper meaning, the reign of the King would be unfavorable and such a King must be Killed by the gods within seven days on the throne, the tension was high as the new King walked with a blindfold scarf on his young face to select one of the three calabashes that would determine his reign.

The atmosphere was tensed, the crowd felt it too more than the young King himself who just saw everything more like a video game or why would the life or the reign of a king be determined in the mischievous through the three calabashes?

Unknown to the crowd, the new King had a dream a night before the event, in which his late grandfather, the former king had appeared to him, he was excited with the young Prince and glad his people finally obeyed the gods, he counseled the prince to select the calabash on his right hand, never take the calabash on the left, he was warned.

In his dream, the late king took his grandson round the city and was told when things ever become difficult for him on the throne and in search for any solution, the black feathers behind the seat of his throne would provide solution to all his worries.

How? He asked.

Grandfather said when the need for it happened it would be clearer to him. It was when he woke up and the revelation in the dream became clearer even with the scarf on his face, it was like his eyes were open, then he remembers what the grandfather said.

He walked as if his eyes were still opened and when he bent down to pick the calabash, he did exactly as he was told in the dream, he picked the one on his right hand. It was then the Chief Priest emerged and opened the calabash for the people to see.

The crowd were happy, the new King picked the calash with honey and his reign would signify sweetness and opportunities for the people of Ovambo.

The happiest couple in the crowd was the parents of the new Kings, they were the first to greet the new King with prayers according to the tradition, the King before he placed the Calabash of honey before the shrine in the Palace with it, he must greet his parents as son for the last time after which the rest of the community will have prostrate to him.

And he must never sit in a function in public with his parents for the rest of his reign, his parents wanted to see him it must be done in the private far away in the eyes of the public.

Chapter

36

Those who refused to obey the warning of the Oracle never escaped the punishment. Before Marie left for Ghana to appease the gods, she was warned never to have carnal relationship with Prince Shogun until all the ritual had been completed.

Unfortunately, she allowed her weakness to override the warning, she disregarded the Oracle and more than two nights it was like she never took the warning signs serious. She could have been delt with in Ghana, but the Oracle knew why the gods spared her life, they wanted her to witness the coronation of her son Mavuso as King in Africa.

Oracle could not persuade gods to forget the repercussion of that disobedience, no matter the sacrifice, just as Marie was sleeping beside Prince Shogun, the black Cobra snake, she had seen in her dreams appeared to her in real life, the presence of the snake was the symbol of annoyance of the gods.

The Cobra snake went for tip of her nose, her eyes and on the mouth several I times until it went for her breast which quickly affected her heart, by the time the family and the new King could see his mother in the morning she was dead and the sight of her face was horrible for the public to comprehend.

Marie's death was a big blow to the new King and his father who had though he was going to have a new beginning with Marie he had married for their son could be crowned not knowing he too had just forty-eight hours more to live.

How did he die?

Somehow after the death of Marie, unexpected thing happened, Professor Bimbo who had remained deaf and dump since he had tried to rescue the little boy from the pool in the United States of America three years ago in which his friend died, suddenly regained his speech and he could also hear as if nothing ever happened to him.

It was indeed the reconciliation between the gods in Ghana and that of Nigeria unlike what would happen to Prince Shogun who just lost his wife Marie, by the time he went to bed 48 hours after the demise of Marie, the black snake was there on the bed with all its fangs.

THE END

Acknowledgements

I will like to show my appreciation to my wife Erelu Chief Mrs. Helyn Sowunmi who encouraged me to finish this book as I was almost got distracted with other projects, however with her support I kept some sleepless nights to think how this book would end, and it did.

Thank you.

Zents Sowunmi is a New York based writer, and also the author of "*The Secrets of Gabriel*" He worked for the Department of Defense Warrior Transition Battalion of the United States Army Fort Bliss, Texas.

Zents is one of the world's favorite storytellers. His books are published in English, Zents holds an MBA and several certifications. He is the author of *Before the Journey Became Home, The Vultures and Vulnerable, 100 ways to Laugh and Unequally Yoking, the secrets of Gabriel* among others and is also completing work on several other publications.

Zents Kunle Sowunmi books are available worldwide. For more information on the author or to purchase autographed copies, please contact the author Zents@korlokipublishers.com.

Available in Large print and as an e-book